SÉANCE ON
A WET
AFTERNOON

SÉANCE ON
A WET
AFTERNOON

MARK McSHANE

MYSTERIOUSPRESS.COM

OPEN ROAD
INTEGRATED MEDIA
NEW YORK

Cover design by Jason Gabbert

ISBN 978-1-4532-3675-8

This 2013 edition published by MysteriousPress.com/Open Road Integrated Media, Inc.
345 Hudson Street
New York, NY 10014
www.mysteriouspress.com
www.openroadmedia.com

SÉANCE ON
A WET
AFTERNOON

One

MYRA STOOD AND WATCHED her husband's motor-cycle and side-car bounce and sway up the unmade, mud-and-rock road and disappear around the corner of the street, then she went back into the house, shivering her shoulders at the March wind. She felt excited and a little bit frightened.

After straightening with her toe the square of unbordered carpet set in front of the door, she went down past the stairs and entered the long narrow kitchen. Working quickly and deftly she began to wash the dishes from lunch.

She was small and thin, narrow across the shoulders and hips, but with surprisingly heavy legs. Her face was plain, cosmetically innocent, and looked a little more than her forty-four years; it had a pointed chin and a sharp-pointed nose, pronounced cheekbones and a high smooth forehead; at the top of the forehead, in the centre, was a tiny star-shaped scar. Between the thick masculine eyebrows and the thick elongated bags of flesh, her eyes shone darkly from their deep setting; shone with a searching intensity that wasn't quite normal. Her mouth was small, and expressed nothing, and above it several deeply cut shadow-holding lines went up halfway to her nostrils and looked almost like a sparse but heavy-bristled moustache. Speckled grey, white and black hair was drawn back not too tightly, or tidily, into a bun that sat close to the crown of her head, but a bit off-centre. She was wearing a grey woollen dress that hung loosely, and sagged on her chest where there was little to fill it out.

As she stood at the sink she glanced up occasionally to look through the window, seeing the long garden, and the unattractive wasteland beyond the broken, unpainted fence, the backs of the semi-detached houses—identical with her own—on the right and the distant brickworks on the left. But she was only vaguely aware of what she saw. Every time she looked up she thought of Bill, her husband, and just where he'd be now, on his journey from the north-east of London to the north-west. As she dried the last cup she thought, *Enfield*, and shuddered at the tingle that ran up her spine.

She left the kitchen by a different door from the one by which she'd entered, and came into the lounge, the only other downstairs room. It was fairly large and almost square, and its walls were the same distempered green that covered every wall in the house. At one side was a fireplace of mottled fawn tile, and at the other a cream door leading to the hall. The furniture was shabby. In the centre of the hardcord carpet was a dining-table and four chairs; in the centre of the table was a wooden fruit bowl which held one shrivelled apple. Two big blue armchairs were huddled on to the balding black hearth-rug, and their larger counterpart was set beneath the window.

Myra stood in front of the couch, her arms folded, each hand gently kneading a bicep, and looked through the net curtains. There was no opposing row of houses, though it was possible to discern traces of long-deserted foundations, and the view was almost identical with that from the back window: five or six square miles of low, rather swampy ground, broken here and there by a heap of rubble, with distant buildings on one side and the back of the housing estate on the other. She thought, *Cockfosters*, and got the tingle again.

She lifted her eyes to the ceiling. Her husband had checked all round after lunch, and just before he'd left they had checked together. But she thought it wouldn't hurt to check again; everything had to be perfect.

She went out into the hall and up the stairs. On the landing she hesitated, then went into the room above the lounge, thinking that a few minutes of quiet meditation would settle her nervousness and ease the uncomfortable flutters of her heart.

The room had no curtains, carpets or linoleum, and the bulb in the ceiling fixture was unshaded. There was a plain deal table, six feet by three, in the middle of the unstained floor, and standing against the back wall were twelve straight chairs. Above the window was a roller blind. This was the seance room.

She carried a chair to the head of the table and sat down, clasping her hands in her lap and closing her eyes. She began to relax, starting from her toes and working slowly up. When her head sagged to one side on the loosened neck she turned her mind to the picture that she always found equally good at inducing sleep or quietude: a tree; a luscious green, sweeping, falling, grass-tickling willow tree of which only the lazy leaves and slumber-heavy boughs were visible, curving up from the centre parting, then over and down to the ground. The picture came quickly, and she sighed, and began to feel calmer at once.

Myra was a sensitive, a medium, a para-normal. And a genuine one; she believed in what she did. She was a rarity among those of her profession, in that she didn't have the usual curtained cabinet, or use trumpets, tambourines, guitars or any of the trappings synonymous with spiritualism; at her séances there were no table-movings or raps or materializations; she didn't even have a spirit control. But she understood why many sensitives, even highly gifted ones, employed all the fancywork; the public wanted a show, and even a medium has to live. But Myra wouldn't, couldn't stoop to it, though she was sure that these manifestations sometimes had supranormal causation. She wanted no hint of charlatanism connected with her work. It was sacred to her.

She was genuine, too, in so far as she never claimed communication with the dead. Not that she actively disclaimed it; she merely replied, when asked whence came her messages, that she didn't know. She did know, but felt it would be being pointlessly honest to tell. She knew that when she sat in trance in physical contact with a client who had the metagnomy to be an agent—and she could sense this in a person, even at a distance—the messages she received, translated into words from the symbols that oozed up from her subliminal, came not from the deceased relative of the client, but from the client's own mind. It was telepathy. But since she was able to mention things known only to the client and the deceased, it was assumed to be communication with the dead. And she didn't discourage the assumption.

But she believed in discarnate agency. She believed fervently, with her heart and soul and intellect. It was her only faith. Her one single ambition and main goal in life was, and had been for twenty years, to justify this belief with fact, with fact produced by herself, for that was the only kind she could accept as absolute. Ever since the realization at thirteen that she possessed extrasensory-perception she had been irresistibly drawn in this one direction. She was consumed by it, always.

And it was to aid her ambition that the Plan had been formed, the one her husband had gone to set in motion.

If successful, the Plan would bring two things: money and notoriety. Myra was not particularly interested in the former; she was satisfied with the bare living her thrice-weekly séances brought in; she was even satisfied with the house—though she realized its lack of 'atmosphere'—and its situation suited her perfectly, being isolated as it was at the very end of a long row. Fame didn't interest her either; in fact, she viewed it with distaste, and connected it with the more drum-beating variety of medium. But it was fame she hoped for, for from it would come reputation. Her fame might last only a week in the mind of the public, but in the minds of those interested in and active in psychic research it would last for ever. She would be established as a sensitive of the first order. The fact that her reputation would rest on a fraud didn't disturb her. It was cheating for an honourable end.

Once established she would come into contact with mediums whose gifts equalled or surpassed her own, and she would be on the road to success. It was, she felt, a case of many minds being better than one. An organized series of séances, each one held with different sensitives, would be sure to take her close to, and perhaps across, the bourne of nature. Too, she wanted to make a solidly welded *rapport* with an older para-normal, one almost ready for the journey beyond the veil, who would, having taken the journey, be an entity to reach for on the other side.

The results of the Plan would enable her to do these things without first having to prove herself. On trial, she always failed. In tests with Zener cards, conducted by various organizations for psychical research, she had never scored above the chance average—though she scored well above in private tests. She found it next to impossible to work with anything but complete acceptance;any scepticism, no matter how mild or sympathetic, froze her. No true artist can accept or understand anything other than an admiring attitude to his work. And Myra was a true artist.

She had not been the seventh child of a seventh child, but she had come into the world with her face covered with a thin veil of skin, which rare occurrence is said by old wives to be a sure sign that the infant is endowed with the gift of second-sight. Her mother scoffed publicly at old wives' tales, and privately believed them, and had waited impatiently for the supernatural phenomena to begin. But it was many years before they did. It wasn't until Myra was entering puberty that she was petrified, then puzzled, then exhilarated by the discovery that she was 'different'. One day she saw her father coming down the street, and went to meet him and held his hand all the way to their house, where she ran in ahead to tell her mother that her father was home for dinner. Only when she was standing in the kitchen doorway did she remember that her father had been dead for six months. It was the first and last time she experienced a materialization, but through the years she produced phenomena of many kinds. After one of the last exams she sat for at the grammar school she had the strange conviction that she would be placed third; strange because she was normally at the bottom of the class. She was placed third. She dreamt of being in a car, surrounded by brightly burning people, and the next day walked to her secretarial job instead of going by bus as she usually did; the bus she should have taken had an accident and burst into flame, and every passenger was severely burned. She dreamt of chasing a white rabbit around a circus ring, and several days later an old friend of the family, a professional conjurer who was playing the local music hall, called at the house and mentioned during the conversation that he was looking for a second assistant. Myra asked for the job, and got it. She was on-stage at Glasgow, now first assistant, when she saw beyond the footlights a vivid picture of her mother sliding head first down a ladder; the picture was as clear and unmysterious as though it were being shown on a cinema screen. She ran to the wings and phoned a neighbour at home, and learned that

9

her mother had been found five minutes before, dying; she had slipped on the ice-covered doorstep and fractured her skull. The phenomena continued.

Eventually Myra left the conjurer, and, because of her stage experience with him, got employment as a clairvoyant's aid. She soon discovered that her employer was a complete fraud, and not the least bit psychic. This, her first taste of professional mediumship, was a bitter disillusionment; but, because she wanted to learn method and procedure, having decided that therein lay her calling, she stayed on, and even helped in the object-moving and cheesecloth-waving. However, she soon sickened of it, and left to start up for herself. She rented a small flat, and became a medium. She failed; youngish unmarried spiritualists who didn't use any of the expected trimmings were not popular. She carried on for several years, holding weekly, poorly attended séances, and working in a factory to support herself. Then she got back into show business, of a sort. She answered the advertisement of a mind reader who wanted an assistant with theatrical experience. The mind reader turned out to be an old woman who travelled the southern fairground circuit and whose telepathy consisted of naming and describing objects given to the assistant by members of the tent audience; this was done by means of a simple code. Myra took the job anyway, and learned the code in two days. For five years she spent her summers on the road and her winters in London, sharing a bed-sitter. Half-way through the sixth summer the old mind reader died, and Myra was surprised to find herself the sole heir. The inheritance consisted mainly of a fairly good tent and a decrepit caravan-bus. Soon thereafter she met Bill, and, mainly because he was the first to have asked her, married him. At the end of the season she cashed her assets and took a mortgage on the house. She became a medium again; and was failing again.

It was the temperature of the séance room that woke her from her soothing reverie. Her feet became cold, the picture disintegrated, and she snapped up with a little straightening jerk of her head.

As she put the chair back in its place she glanced up at the wall, at a picture. It was a foot-square thinly framed composition of bits of plain and coloured glass, mirror and tinfoil. She smiled fondly at it, and thought of her husband, then thought of his journey to Barnet, but now without the tingle of excitement and fear.

She went out on to the landing, then into the back bedroom. The only light came from behind her, from the high, cobwebby window that faced the landing, but it was enough to suit her purpose. She looked first to the far side of the room, where there was a double bed, a small cupboard and a chair, all painted white; the bed was turned down, and lying on it was a small pink nightdress. The window was completely covered by a large sheet of clean new plywood, no daylight showing around its edges. The carpet, almost wall-to-wall, was laid facedown and its pattern and basic colour were impossible to discern. On the wall opposite the window was a picture identical with that in the séance room.

She nodded at everything, checked the key to see that the lock worked smoothly and quietly, then backed out. She pushed open the bathroom door to look briefly at the plywood over the window, and nodded again and went downstairs. Back in the lounge she crossed to the frontof the couch and stood looking out at the grey afternoon.

Everything, she thought, was ready. Both back windows were correctly boarded, with the boards undetectable from outside, behind the net curtains in one and the frosted glass in the other; the bedroom looked sufficiently bare and antiseptic; the peep-hole for looking through into the séance room was fixed to be used the other way, too, for observation. And the circumstances were favourable; the lonely situation of the house, and the fact that the house next door was empty, up for sale. Number sixty Josephine Avenue was ready for its guest.

She went and sat in one of the blue armchairs, pulling back the hem of her dress, baring her knees to the fire, and waited; she waited for her husband to come back with the little girl he had gone to kidnap.

Bill didn't use his old motor-bike very often, but whenever he did he drove it as he drove now, at a circumspect thirty, with one hand steering and the other resting on the waterproof that was snapped down tightly across the top of the side-car, as though the two parts of the machine had to be held together. It was the attitude of a man too old and nervous for driving. But Bill wasn't old. He was thirty-nine, five years younger than his wife. He was also a stone lighter than his wife, and only a couple of inches taller—a little below average. He had round shoulders and lumpy-knuckled hands, thin arms and legs and a sunken chest. His face, which had the faintly sad, rather apologetic expression of the valetudinarian, was dominated by the nose: long and flat and smooth, its tip considerably lower than the nostrils, the type of nose often paired with a hare lip, it seemed to be poised in perpetual crouch, tensely waiting to leap away from the small pale eyes and puffy mouth; it was red and shiny from September to April, and was very red now, being the only part of the face showing between the scarf above the trench coat collar and the fur-edged goggles beneath the white crash helmet.

Bill had asthma, rheumatism and migraine. He hadn't worked in winter for many years, and wasn't working now, though the stirrings of spring had started him searching vaguely for a job, one as light as his numerous illness-lost other jobs had been. His favourite was a driving instructor; but it seemed to be the favourite of many. He would have been quite happy to stay home altogether, except that his conscience bothered him; Myra didn't mind supporting them both with the proceeds from her séances, but he minded. However, his conscience wouldn't be able to murmur against his living on the cash benefits that would be a part of the success of the Plan, since he was doing the major implementations himself.

He wasn't thinking about the Plan at the moment; he wasn't allowing himself to. He knew that if he did think about it he'd turn round and go home. Considered vaguely as *the Plan*, it was all right, thrilling even; but thought on, chewed over, examined without optimism, its possible ramifications followed, it became a monstrous, preposterous, terrifying thing. When, during a discussion with his wife on her mediumistic future, he'd put forward the idea of a kidnapping, he hadn't been serious and had expected a laugh. Myra hadn't laughed; and here he was, three weeks later, not laughing either.

He noticed that he was approaching the outskirts of Barnet, and slowed a little and moved to the outside traffic lane, ignoring the impatient blasting of a horn behind, and began to watch the streets on the right. He saw the one he wanted, and after looking in the large rear-view mirror and checking its picture by glancing back, he turned off the main road and drove down a residential street that was lined with high precision-clipped hedges, slowing his speed to a quietly chugging fifteen. The street was deserted.

At the bottom the road turned sharply to the left. Bill swung to the right, into a narrow dirt lane running between even higher but less neatly clipped privet, and reduced speed still more.

There was a bend, and suddenly he was out of the lane and in open country, in fields that stretched away, rising gently, to a distant wood. Fifty yards in front of him was a shabby wooden building the size of a bungalow. Behind him, more high privet, with scattered rooftops just visible above it.

He rolled slowly and squeakily across the grass and around to the other side of the large hut, where there was a veranda and a padlocked door that said *Happy Boys' Cricket Club*. He stopped and switched off the ignition. The engine coughed into silence, and he sat perfectly still, listening. It was very quiet. He got off the bike.

After glancing at his wrist-watch he took off his helmet, goggles and gloves, and sat them on the saddle while he unsnapped a corner of the waterproof. He slipped his things in the side-car, and secured the cover.

Moving back to the other side of the machine he bent to the mirror and looked at his hair, the arrangement of which constituted his disguise. Normally it stood fluffily high, carelessly waved, and was soft, silky and dark brown, and rather romantic—though he was completely unaware of this. Now it was black with grease, parted down the centre and brushed flat to his skull. The change made a great difference. He looked older, his face more square, and his nose, without the counterbalance of the tall quiff, looked much longer and its flatness was more pronounced. He also looked tougher, but still not tough.

He turned and walked away, pulling the scarf down from his mouth and settling it at his throat. He went back to the lane and down it and came out on the street, which, he was glad to see, was still deserted. He headed toward the main road, walking at a steady pace, his feet turning inward slightly. A tightness of anxiety began to develop around his heart, and he compressed his lips.

When he was near the end of the street a tall woman appeared abruptly from a gateway and stopped directly in his path. He averted his face and detoured to the edge of the pavement. The woman glanced at him, then lowered a small Pekingese to the ground and started to make high-pitched cries at it. Bill passed her, quickening his step, and was unable to resist looking back. She was giving all her attention to the dog, but he didn't feel happy till he'd reached the main road and turned the corner.

He walked for ten minutes, unconcerned now by the people about; there were too many for him to be noticed. After trotting across the road, briskly among the traffic, he went into a wide street of large, bleak, Gothic-Victorian houses, and soon was moving along beside a low wall of new brick that was topped by tall and heavy railings. Behind the rails, and in places sticking through them, were young coniferous trees, planted closely at set intervals and a uniform six feet in height.

He slowed, making a show of frowning and putting his hands in his coat pockets, as though searching for something he had just thought he might have left behind, then came to a stop level with a place where three of the rails were missing. Taking his hands from his pockets and patting his chest, he looked around. There was one man, his back turned, painting a gate farther along on the opposite side of the street, and two men were standing talking on a corner about thirty yards away. A young woman in nursemaid's uniform was coming along briskly from the main road, and Bill stood still, patting his coat, till she'd passed.

Moving slowly, and with his eyes flitting back and forth from the two men to the gate painter, he edged close to the low wall and placed one foot on it. He grasped a rail, paused, and jerked himself quickly through the opening and into the trees. With one hand held protectively before his face and the other stretched out leading the way he pushed through the interlocking branches, blinking rapidly at the foliage that swept by.

The trees ended after three yards and he was standing close against a shed. The boards were widely spaced and between them he could see a clutter of bicycles. He moved to the corner of the shed and looked cautiously around it. Beyond an area of gravel was a large house, old looking and predominantly dark grey stone, but with here and there among its many roofs and angles jutting bluffs of new brick. There was the faint sound of children's voices.

He withdrew his head and leaned on the boards to wait. He asked himself if he was frightened, and decided at once that he was, but not greatly so; at this stage a plausible explanation would probably suffice if things went wrong. But, he thought, looking at his wrist-watch, in ten minutes it would be too late for explanations.

His heart began to trip faster, and he quickly turned his mind to pleasanter things, to the future, the bright future after the Plan.

To Bill, a bright future meant his wife's future. He had no ambitions, as such, of his own; he merely thought of things being better, meaning living in a centrally heated house, one with no damp patches on the walls, and being untroubled by debts and the necessity to work. But for his wife he was very ambitious. In the six years since their marriage his admiration for her had increased greatly. When they had met, she with her fairground mind-reading act and he applying for the job as the ticket seller, he'd thought of her as a theatrical, an artiste, and hadn't understood her explanations of what she was trying to do. He still didn't understand, completely, but was now convinced of her greatness; convinced by her proven

ability, her sincerity, intenseness and lack of interest in mate-
rial things. Even though he had no awareness beyond normal
intelligence himself—and this he regretted—the infectious-
ness of his wife's zeal and dedication had drawn him into
psychical research, and he read about it constantly, and had
been allowed to make for himself a peep-hole through which
he could watch the séances. He looked forward confidently
to the day when his wife would be the first to prove beyond
all doubt to the hard world of science that communication
with the dead was an actuality; when the name of Myra Savage would be pronounced with awe; when she would be hon-
oured everywhere as the one who had found a way across the
greatest frontier of all.

And when that day came, he thought, he'd scoff at the
memory of the worries, doubts and fears he'd had about the
Plan, which, after all, was what had made the whole thing
possible, and be ashamed that he was ever reluctant to go
through with it.

A bell rang loudly, and he pushed himself quickly erect
from the side of the shed and went back into the trees, feeling
a tightness forming low down in his throat. When he judged
himself to be within a yard or so of the railings he turned
left and moved along parallel with them. He went swiftly but
carefully, making as little noise as possible with the foliage.

Presently he glimpsed an opening ahead, where a gravel
driveway cut through the trees, and he moved to the right,
looking now at the ground, searching for the marks he had
made on his last reconnaissance. He came to a spot that was
trampled smooth, and stood on it.

He was now in a perfect position for observation. Through small gaps between branches he had a clear view of the gravel path three feet away, and the imposing entrance of the house at its end and the large gateway on his immediate right. On the other side of the drive was a board, set at an angle, saying *Clement's Day School For Young Ladies.*

He'd had surprisingly little trouble in arranging the first part of the Plan, choosing place and person. Clement's, because it was far from Josephine Avenue, and because he was fairly familiar with the neighbourhood, having once been for a short time a cab driver in Barnet, was the first school he had tried. He'd dawdled around outside, watching the pupils leave, and saw many leave in cars, one a chauffeured Bentley. After four visits to the school, spread over two weeks, he'd found out that the Bentley belonged to a Charles Clayton, a wealthy industrialist; and he had seen that the pick-up of Clayton's only child always followed the same pattern: the chauffeur drove to the gate and waited till the girl appeared, then got out and ushered her ceremoniously into the rear; and always the engine was left running.

There was a bang, and a babble of young voices. Bill tensed, his buttocks clenching. A group of girls, ranging from small five-year-olds to hefty thirteens, had come pouring out of the house. They all wore the same dark green coats and berets and long brown stockings. Some turned and moved out of sight, going, Bill knew, to the cycle shed, and others walked past his hiding place and out of the gate. As he watched them go, the Bentley swished up quietly and stopped at the kerb.

Now he began to feel scared, and hot. He licked his lips and looked back to the house.

More girls came out, some boisterously, chasing quickly down the path and squealing, others sedately and solemn-faced, walking in twos and threes and talking. He saw the Clayton child. She came out alone, pulling a beret on to her straight black hair. She was six years old, small and pale.

The chauffeur got out at the far side of the car, came around in front of it and swung wide the rear door. He was middle-aged and thick-set and had a hairline moustache. The girl smiled and broke into a skip.

When she'd passed him, Bill moved quickly, nervously to the edge of the path. Another passing girl looked up at him, frowned distantly, and walked on.

The Clayton child got inside the car and the chauffeur closed the door, carefully and bowing a little. Bill stepped out on to the gravel, walked quickly through the gate and stopped behind the chauffeur. His heart was thudding and the insides of his clenched fists were damp. He said, 'Excuse me.'

The chauffeur turned, the smile for the little girl still on his face. 'Yes?'

'Are you Mr. Clayton's man?'

'Yes.'

Bill cleared his throat, and, shakily, pronounced the long-practised sentence: 'The headmistress has a letter for you which she would like you to give to your employer.'

The man half lifted his hand. 'Very good.'

'No. I mean, she has it. The headmistress has it. She wants to give it you in person . . . you know.'

'Oh.' The man frowned slightly, and lowered his hand.

'She wants you to go to her office now,' Bill said quickly, too quickly, 'so she can give it you—er—now.'

The chauffeur glanced at the car. Bill said, 'It's just through the main door, her office, and up the stairs.' He thought the man was about to refuse to go, and suddenly, inexplicably, hoped he would.

The chauffeur nodded. 'Righto. Thanks.' He skirted around Bill and walked through the gateway. Bill turned and watched. When he saw the man go inside the house he went quickly round to the other side of the car, his legs trembling and uncertain.

He tried twice, rapidly, to open the car door, but his hand was so wet with sweat it flew down off the handle as soon as he'd lowered it. With the third, less frantic attempt, he got it open and scrambled inside.

Putting the automatic transmission into drive he pressed down on the accelerator. The car jerked, stopped, and the engine went dead. He shuddered and closed his eyes, but opened them again at once. He saw that the hand brake was still on and pressed the button to release it.

He didn't know which was the starter. He searched the dashboard frantically, panic rising at speed, his fingers dithering over the bewildering array of buttons and knobs. Just when he'd made up his mind to leave the car and run, he found it.

He pushed the button. Nothing happened. He couldn't stop the little cry he made with the sharp jerk in of breath. Then he saw the trouble. He slipped the transmission into neutral and tried the starter again. There was a short whine, and the engine hummed.

He banged the lever into drive and flattened the accelerator and the car shot away from the kerb. He didn't look back.

Doing fifty miles an hour he reached the end of the street and with only a slight reduction of speed made a right-hand turn on to the main road. A car coming from the left squealed its brakes wildly. Bill pressed his foot down and passed another car, on the wrong side of the road. He had originally planned to take a circuitous route back to the field, but now he'd forgotten that; he wanted to get to his bike, then to his home.

He glanced up at the mirror, and was startled to see a close-up of the girl's face. She was standing right behind him, her nose flattened whitely on the glass partition. She looked intrigued. Her eyes met his in the mirror, and he looked away.

Ahead the traffic was slowing, lining up behind a stopped bus. When, his stomach tightening, he had almost reached the back of the queue, the bus moved on, and the traffic with it.

He saw his street on the left, and slowed, and swung into it at a normal speed. A man and woman were walking towards him, but they were talking busily and didn't give him so much as a glance. As he turned at the mouth of the lane he looked back at the main road. All was quiet.

Even though it wasn't his car, and even though his mind was a gabble of excited, frightened thoughts, he still winced as the hedges scraped and squeaked on the coachwork at either side. Out of the lane the Bentley bounced smoothly across the grass. He steered around the hut, came to a sudden stop behind his machine, switched off the ignition, and sagged back in the seat and closed his eyes. He felt surprised to find himself back where he'd started. Everything seemed a little unreal.

There was a faint thud from behind, and he twisted round. The girl was sitting neatly in the centre of the seat, her hands in her lap. She was watching him curiously. He got out of the car and went to his bike. Turning so that he could keep an eye on the girl he unsnapped the cover of the side-car and took out his helmet, goggles and gloves, and put them on quickly, then strode back to the Bentley.

He twisted the handle of the rear door, and pulled. The door didn't move; it was locked. He glanced sharply at the girl. She smiled slightly, her lips together. He hurried round to the other side. That door was also locked. The girl's smile widened, showing a row of space between her eye teeth.

He looked around helplessly, the panic rising in him again. He hadn't expected anything like this. An hysterical infant, yes; a grinning schemer, no. He rapped on the window, and said, 'Open the door.'

She shook her head.

He forced a smile to his lips and put his head friendlily on one side. 'Come on now, open the door.'

Another shake.

'I've—er—got some ice-cream.'

She giggled, and shook her head more vigorously, her short hair whipping across her face.

He looked down longingly at the locking catch on the inside sill, then replaced his smile with a scowl, rapped on the window again, hard, and said sternly, 'Open up at once,' and added, plaintively, 'there's a good girl.'

He jumped. A bell had sounded, and seemed quite close. Gripping his hands together he walked nervously to his bike, passed around it, walked back to the car, circled it, went round the bike again and stopped at the driver's side of the Bentley. He opened the front door and felt the thick glass of the partition, and suddenly twisted to face the dashboard. One of the buttons was marked *P*. He jabbed at it, turning back to face the rear. There was a hum, and the partition began to slide down.

The girl's smile vanished and she scrambled to the arm rest. The partition stopped, but it had already dropped half-way. Keeping a finger on the button Bill stretched his free arm through the opening and released the sill catch, then quickly reached outside and opened the door. His eyelids sagging with relief, he swung wide the door and said, 'All right. Come on.'

The child pressed herself into the far corner and stared at him sullenly. He put one foot inside the car, leaned forward and grabbed her arm. She kicked him on the elbow, but he hardly felt it. As he pulled her, squirming, out on to the grass, the bell sounded again, and this time it seemed closer.

He ran to the bike, dragging the girl behind him, and heard her say, 'You wait. I'll tell.'

He shoved her up against the side-car and gave her a little shake, and hissed, 'Now stand still.'

'Shan't.' She kicked him on the ankle. 'I'll tell.'

Gasping at the pain he pressed his body against her and

kept her held firmly while he reached in the side-car and brought out a bottle and a pad of white cloth.

The girl suddenly began wailing, stridently and without emotion; it sounded like a jammed horn on a car.

He said, 'Quiet, quiet,' and hastily uncapped the bottle and spilled a drop of the chloroform on to the pad. He hesitated, then added some more. After capping the bottle and throwing it in the side-car he stood back from the girl and bent down.

She tried lustily to twist her face away, going from side to side and up and down, and her beret fell off, but he managed to get the pad over her nose and mouth and keep it there. There was another moment of fierce struggle, then her movements became weak and sluggish and she sagged at the knees. Her eyes opened and closed slowly.

He withdrew the pad. She yawned, looked at him sleepily, and opened her mouth as though to speak. He returned the pad. In a few seconds she slumped against his arm, unconscious. He laid her carefully in the side-car, threw in the pad and beret, and roughly fastened down the cover.

Hurrying to the Bentley he used his gloved hands to wipe every spot he'd touched or thought he'd touched. The bell rang again, but faintly. He gave the sound a trembly smile, feeling more confident now and less frightened. He thought that with everything going wrong to start with, it would be more than likely that from here on things would go right.

He went back to the bike and swung into the saddle. The engine started at the first kick, and his morale took an upward surge; all along he'd had a fear that the engine would give him trouble. Looking at his watch as he moved off he saw that it was twelve minutes since he'd left the school.

He headed across the centre of the field, away from the hut and the lane, going quickly at first but then slowing a little as the side-car began to bounce. In a corner of the field was a gate. He jumped down and opened it, and drove on, feeling a slight pang at not having closed it again. As he turned on to a rough track running beside deep plough ruts, he looked back, and saw that the Bentley was just as he'd left it, its doors hanging open. He thought it quite possible for several hours to pass before the car was found.

He went through another gate, across a large meadow—stampeding a herd of bag-hanging cows—over a shaky plank bridge, through two more gates, and came out on to a cindered lane that rose toward a wood on the brow of a hill. He put on speed, reached the wood, circled it and was out of sight of the Bentley, the cricket pavilion, and Barnet.

The lane stretched away below him, dead straight, and at the bottom of it was a tarmac road. He knew he was safe now; the road had no main connexion with Barnet, and would have no check points put on it should the police decide to throw a cordon around the town. He sped downhill, and the last vestige of fear and worry was soothed away by the barking monody of his engine. In an hour he would be home.

Bill came into the hall and closed the living-room door softly behind him, and, after pausing to button up the jacket of his baggy clerical grey suit, went quietly up the stairs. His hair had been washed, and dried by the fire, and was now its usual shape, waving loose and high on his head. As he reached the landing he belched, and patted his mouth and murmured, 'Par' me.'

He stopped outside the door of the back bedroom and put his head close to it to listen. He could hear nothing. Moving to the side he went into the séance room, to the centre of the row of chairs, stepping lightly on the bare boards. He rested his knee on a chair and reached up to the picture and pushed it gently to the side. It slid round, flat against the wall, till it was upside down, and stayed there of its own accord. In the middle of the unfaded square of green distemper was a clean-cut hole, an inch across, through which came a glimmer of light. He closed with the hole and put his eye right on it.

The ceiling fixture in the bedroom had an unusually low-watt bulb and the peep-hole didn't allow a wall-to-wall view; he was able to see only the dim lower half of a lump on the bed; but the lump was perfectly still, and that was all he wanted to know. He nodded, and slid the picture back into place.

When he went back into the living-room his wife looked around from her seat by the fire. 'Still asleep?'

'Yes. Quiet as a mouse.' He was about to cross to the hearth when he heard a whistled tune from the street.

Myra said, 'Paper boy?'

Bill looked out of the window and saw a figure sweep by in the darkening light. 'Yes, that's him.' He turned and went back to the hall.

The front door was made of nine-inch-square panes of frosted glass, except for a foot of wood along the bottom that held the letter slot. The whistling grew louder and a mottled shape appeared on the door. A moment later a rolled newspaper shot with a bang half-way through the slot. Bill pulled it out and quickly opened it to scan the front page.

Myra called, 'Anything?'

He returned to the lounge, looking at the paper and shaking his head. 'No, doesn't seem to be. Can't really expect it yet.' He flipped through to the back page. 'It was only a couple of hours ago after all.'

Myra came across, closed the door, switched on the light, took the paper from him and began to go through it. She said, 'It is getting dark. I think we had better have the curtains drawn.' Her voice was low and pleasant, and her diction, formed unconsciously from years of having to be heard and understood clearly the first time round, precise and perfect; she never, ever, contracted words. With her unplaceable, accentless accent and too perfect use of English she sounded like one to whom the language is not native.

Bill knelt on the couch and drew across the flimsy green curtains, pulling them tight and keeping them together in the middle by skewering the cloth with a black-knobbed hatpin. The curtains dragged back from the fastening, leaving a thin shaft of window above and below it.

Myra dropped the paper on the table and returned to her seat on the left of the hearth. Bill took the other armchair, and they both leaned forward, forearms on knees, staring into the glowing fire.

After a while Myra said, 'They will know by now, of course.'

'Oh yes. Probably five minutes after I'd gone. I told you about those bells I heard. In fact, I'll bet we find out later that the police threw road-blocks all around Barnet within ten minutes of me leaving the school.'

'It will be in the paper tomorrow morning.'

'Sure to be.'

They fell silent again. Myra tapped at the fire with a partly chromed poker and broke up the neat mound of coals, causing Bill to frown slightly. The blue-faced clock on the mantel ticked loudly, and every now and then gave a dull click.

Myra hung the poker on its rack and turned to look at her husband. 'Well. Now we start on part two.'

He said, 'I'll get the letter,' and rose and moved through the narrow space between the armchairs and circled the table.

On one side of the hall door was a well-crammed bookcase; on the window side a small bureau. He pulled down the flap of the bureau and brought out a writing tablet, its face page already covered with pencilled long-hand. He also brought out a sheet of brown paper, a bottle of glue and a pair of scissors, and these he set on the table. Back in his chair he put the tablet on the wide arm and took a pencil from his pocket. 'Right.'

Myra said, 'Read it to me. See how it sounds.'

Bill cleared his throat, and began to read: *'Dear Sir, this . . .'*

'That,' interrupted Myra, 'seems a bit silly.'

'Yes, it does a bit. Too formal.' He struck out the first two words and began again: *'This is to notify you that your little girl is in our possession. She is quite safe, and if you follow instructions properly she will remain safe. When you have read this letter, destroy it. By this time you will have informed the police of your daughter's disappearance. That was to be expected. But do not tell them about*

29

this letter. We are professional criminals and we mean business. You will find enclosed a lock of your daughter's hair, to prove that she really is in our possession. Your instructions are as follows. One. You will put an advert in the personal column of Tuesday's evening Chronicle, *to the effect that you are willing to oblige, and sign it with your Christian name. This advert you will address to Longfellow. Two. You will get a blue overnight bag, bearing the initials of the British Overseas Airways Corporation, and into this bag you will put twenty-five thousand pounds. This sum . . .'* He stopped, and looked at his wife. 'We still don't know if all that money'll go in one of those little bags.'

She frowned at the fire. 'Oh, I think it would.'

'Perhaps we'd better make some of them fivers, instead of all ones.'

'Very well.'

'Say, ten thousand in fivers.'

'Very well.'

He altered the script, and read, *'This sum is to be made up of fifteen thousand in one-pound notes and ten thousand in five-pound notes. You will be informed later, by telephone, where and when you are to deliver the money. After delivery your daughter will be returned to you. But if these instructions are not followed perfectly, or if there is any attempt to detain the man to whom you will give the money, you will never see your daughter alive again. We mean what we say. Signed, Longfellow.'*

Myra said, 'Today is Monday. Will he he able to get an advert in tomorrow's paper?'

'Well, he should get this letter in the morning, or noon at the latest. He'll have time.'

'But we do not want to give him anything to worry about. Better to say Tuesday or Wednesday evening.'

'Right you are.'

'And I think you had better change *lock* of hair. Her hair, you said, was straight. Lock, I think, denotes a curl. Better to say *piece*.'

'Or *some*?'

'*Piece*.'

'Yes, *piece*.' He made the changes, and said, 'Well, that's that then.'

'There is not something we have left out?'

'I don't think so.'

They frowned thoughtfully at one another, each searching the other's face. Bill said, 'No, that's it. You're sure about it being the *Chronicle*?'

'Why not?'

'That's the paper we take. Don't you think it'd be better to have it put in another paper.'

'No. That is carrying caution too far. A million people take the *Chronicle*.'

'Right. I'll get to work then.' He rose and went to the table, and his wife followed. He picked up the scissors and held them out. 'You get the hair, eh?'

'Yes.' She took the scissors and went out of the room.

Bill sat at the table. He opened out the newspaper, laid the tablet beside it, and with his pencil began picking out and marking words in the paper to match those in the letter draught.

Myra clicked on the landing light and went briskly up the

stairs, her breath coming out in faint clouds of vapour. Outside the bedroom door she stopped for a moment to listen, then quietly turned the key in the lock and pushed open the door. The light was depressingly dim, making the room feel colder than it was, and she shivered as she crossed to the bed.

Bending down she gently eased the blankets away from the girl's face. This was her first look at the Clayton child. When Bill had come home from Barnet he'd carried the girl in completely hidden inside a blanket, and had taken her straight upstairs and put her to bed himself, he having the experience that Myra lacked, being the eldest of a large family and she an only child, and childless.

Now she saw with surprise, and a faint tinge of pleasure, that the little girl was plain. The nose was large, the mouth wide and the forehead shallow. Hardly, Myra thought, twenty-five thousand pounds' worth. But there was something about the face that was distinctive; it had a certain determination, and individuality.

Myra lifted a string-thick strand of hair and snipped it off close to the scalp, and made a knot in its centre to hold the hairs together. She went out of the room and carefully locked the door behind her.

Bill had found nearly all the words he wanted. Some he'd had to make up by joining words and part-words. There were two *daughters* in the paper, and he'd made the other two he needed from *laughter*, which he found several times in the political column. Many of the words were of different-sized type, but he felt this was unimportant, as was the haphazard apostrophizing.

His wife came in and silently handed him the scissors, and stood at his side and watched, folding her arms and frowning.

He set to work with the scissors and glue. He cut out the words one at a time and fixed them on the piece of brown paper, which had been lining a drawer for several years. He worked slowly, neatly and carefully, and enjoyed the task, and was a little sorry when he'd finished.

Myra nodded her approval when he held up the letter, and went to the writing-desk and fetched a stamped envelope, home-made out of more brown paper.

With the exception of *street*, every name of the address had to be constructed from part-words, and the finished envelope, to Bill's eye, had an uncomfortable look about it.

The letter was wiped free of possible fingerprints and folded with the snippet of hair inside, then put into the envelope, which was sealed, wiped and placed in a large piece of newsprint.

Bill leaned back, and said, 'There.'

Myra went to the door. 'I will get my coat.' She left the room, and when she returned a minute later was wearing an old-fashioned black coat, waisted and square-shouldered, and under her arm were several folded blankets and a pair of green pyjamas. She said, 'I brought your bedding,' and moved to the couch and dropped her load.

'Yes, thank you.'

She took the letter from him and put it in her pocket, then buttoned up the coat to the neck, lifting back her head. 'It is cold tonight.'

He said, 'I'd go myself. But just after washing my hair . . . you know.'

She smiled slightly. 'It is quite all right. I do not mind.'

'Which way are you going?'

'As was arranged. Bus to the first tube station, then tube to the West End.'

'It'd be just the same if you posted it in Leyton, say, without going all the way in.'

'I think we had better stick to the original idea.'

'Yes, of course.'

They went together into the hall, and Bill switched on the light and opened the front door. It was fully dark out now, and the stream of light from the doorway penetrated no farther than the waist-high wall three feet from the front step.

Myra said, 'Burn the newspaper.'

'I know.'

'It will probably be late when I get back, so you had better not wait up for me.'

'All right. I am a bit tired.'

'See you in the morning then.'

'Yes. Good night.'

Bill kept the door open long enough for his wife to see her way to the pavement, then he closed it and returned to the lounge. After he'd put away the glue and scissors, and burned the shredded newspaper, he began to arrange the blankets on the couch.

He often slept in the living-room in winter; sometimes his asthma was so bad that he found it an ordeal to climb the stairs, and couldn't lie flat in a bed anyway. He spent the nights in his armchair, dozing and keeping the fire alive. He was quite well at the moment, but there was no room for him upstairs; the box-room had only a single bed, and his wife was a restless sleeper, needing space to thresh in.

He stuffed a cushion under the bottom blanket, to serve as a pillow, and he was finished. Crossing to the bookcase he pulled out one of the many Sherlock Holmeses, which he was fond of examining—more than reading—to see if he could come across instances of the author's philosophy. He sat in his chair, spent a moment shaping the fire into a tidy mound, and leaned back with a little sigh of comfort and opened the book.

Ten minutes later he closed the book with a snap and tossed it on to the other chair. He wasn't able to concentrate. He hadn't been able to concentrate, on anything, since the conception of the Plan. There was always a little worry nagging at the back of his mind. It wasn't the implementation itself; he'd done the first of the two major jobs scheduled, and was so pleased with the way he'd succeeded that the fear of doing the second had been reduced; the rest was up to his wife. It wasn't the rights and wrongs of the scheme, now; although he had never in his life knowingly done a wrong thing, he condoned the illegal act because Myra said it was a means to an end that would benefit mankind, and he believed what Myra said; she also said it was only technically illegal, since they had no intentions of keeping the money and the child would be returned safely; she conceded that it was in a way morally wrong to abduct a child, but it was only for three or four days, and there was no question of ill-treatment; it was almost like a little holiday. The thing that worried him was that no one would believe, should they be found out, that they were not real kidnappers, real criminals. It would be assumed, as he himself would assume were he not involved, that the object was gain. The true motive would be scoffed at, as were all things connected with spiritualism.

But, he thought consolingly, the details had been so carefully thought out there was little chance of anything going wrong, and afterwards, after the police had found the child and the money in the disused builder's hut already selected— sent there by Myra, supposedly having seen the place in a vision—there would be little or nothing for the authorities to go on. The girl would be able to describe only a room and, vaguely, a motor-bike and two people. Meanwhile the room would have been returned to its normal state and the cheap white paint removed from the furniture, and the two people would have shed their small but sufficing disguises; the bike was unimportant, being like ten thousand others. And anyway, since the child and money had been recovered, surely the police would slacken off their investigation. And then again, there was the dream.

Myra had had a dream in which she saw herself sitting on a stool in the centre of a ring of men, all old and wearing black wigs, who were shaking their heads in bewilderment and repeating, 'Only you know the truth.' She had translated the dream as meaning the authorities would never know what had happened, unless she or her husband told them.

Which, thought Bill, wasn't very likely. He reached for the book, and settled down again to *The Speckled Band*.

Two

THE BOX-ROOM WAS SMALL, and impossibly crowded. The wardrobe and dressing-table from the back bedroom had been moved in and were cramped at the side and foot of the bed. Since there was no space to open the doors of the wardrobe, all the clothes expected to be needed had been taken out of it and were hanging from its top and scattered round the room from the picture rail.

Myra was asleep, on her side, her legs doubled up, but she suddenly opened her eyes and jerked her legs out straight as the sound of a child crying brought her awake. She yawned and moved over on to her back, snuggling into the blankets, and lay still, listening. She was reluctant to leave the bed; it was a cold morning, and she wasn't thoroughly rested; it had been late when she'd returned from posting the letter in Oxford Circus, and she wasn't used to late nights.

She frowned as the crying continued. But after another moment it stopped, and there were several dull thuds as doors were banged. She supposed her husband was tending to the child, and sighed and relaxed.

She thought that so far everything had gone well. She had never for a minute doubted it would go otherwise, but it had made her nervous for her husband to be alone in Barnet, away from her steadying hand; she knew he was not of strong fibre, and apt to wilt under strain. But he had done very well. The worst part was over, and the rest would be easy.

The door knob squeakily turned, and swung toward her. Bill came in, pressing himself between the door and the wardrobe. He smiled, and whispered, 'Good morning.'

'Good morning. You are dressed.'

'Yes, I've been up for an hour. I didn't sleep very much last night.' He winced. 'That rheumatism . . .'

She nodded brusquely and sat up. She didn't want to hear about his rheumatism. She was sorry about it and was fond of her husband, but she found it impossible to live in the constant state of sympathy his incessant complaints demanded. She asked, 'What happened with the child?'

Frowning at the loudness of her voice he whispered, 'I heard her crying, and came upstairs. She just wanted to go to the bathroom, so I let her.'

'Did she get a good look at you?'

'No. She was still half asleep.'

'What did she say?'

'Well, she was only sort of mumbling. I just understood when she asked where her nanny was.'

'What did you tell her?'

'I didn't answer.'

'Good.' She thought for a moment, before saying, 'I think you can start the breakfast. Scrambled eggs, as arranged. I will take it in and get the meeting over with.'

He nodded, and was retreating when a loud bang sounded from below. They both started, and stared fixedly at one another. Then Bill smiled quickly, said, 'The paper,' and hurried out.

Myra stood up and moved bouncily to the foot of the bed, pulled a bathrobe off a hanger and put it on, got to the floor and hastily stamped into her slippers and squeezed out of the room.

Bill was sitting on the bottom step, the newspaper held before him. Myra sat on the second step and looked over his shoulder. He said, 'Down here. Just that bit.'

At the foot of the page were a few lines of type under the heading, *Girl Missing*. Myra read aloud: '*The only daughter of Charles Clayton, wealthy chairman of Clayton Industries Ltd., was stated last night to be missing from home. Adriana, aged six, disappeared soon after leaving her school near Barnet. A search party was organized.*'

Bill said, 'I thought there'd be more than that.'

'There will be. They probably had not realized what had actually happened.'

'You don't suppose they're going to keep it all secret?'

'No. They just had not thought of an abduction.'

Bill folded the paper and turned to look at his wife. 'But what else could they think?'

'Well, perhaps that it was somebody playing a joke.'

'Hmmm.'

'Or that the man who had taken the car was merely a car thief.'

He nodded. 'Yes, that's likely.'

'It will be in the evening paper. You see.'

'Well there's one thing: we know her name now. Adriana. Posh, eh?'

'Yes.' She rose and turned and began to climb the stairs. 'And so to breakfast.'

Bill went into the lounge, saw that the newly made fire was burning properly, and passed through into the kitchen. As he prepared the scrambled eggs for the girl he reflected that if Clayton kept the affair out of the papers the whole point of it would be lost; there'd be no success without publicity. He sighed, but not unhappily, and told himself it was one more thing to worry about.

Myra had a quick wash and went to her room to dress. First she put on her grey wool, then stood on the bed to reach down a white summer frock, which she also donned. From the dresser's top drawer—the only one that could be opened—she took a large white handkerchief, and carried it to the bathroom. Her hair had not been taken down the night before, and it was only a minute's work to tuck in the strands that had got loose from the bun. When it was neat she fastened the handkerchief over it—nurse-style.

After examining her over-all appearance she moved closer to the mirror and looked dubiously at the scar high on her brow. It was during the hasty removal of the face veil that the scar had been dug. Diamond-shaped at first, the years had blunted the impression of the sides and left it looking like a four-pointed star. It was a valuable asset to a medium when passed off as a birthmark, and discounting a few minutes it was a birthmark. Myra was proud of it. But now the fact of its distinctiveness gave her pause.

She decided to hide it, and rearranged the handkerchief to come down to just above her eyebrows. It was better, she thought, and looked even more nurse-like.

She went downstairs. In the living-room she unpinned the curtains and opened them. It was a tired grey morning with black waterlogged clouds coming in low from the east. She moved to the fire and briefly dry-washed her hands, close to the flames, before going into the kitchen.

Bill looked around from the stove. 'Almost ready.' He grinned. 'Well, you look perfect. Just the job.'

'Think so?'

'Yes, perfect.' He took a pan off the stove and emptied its lumpy contents into a small dish on a tray. Also on the tray was a mug, and a plate of bread and butter.

Myra crossed to him. 'All ready?'

'Almost. Just warming the milk.'

'Oh, there is no need to warm it.'

'Poor little mite needs something warm. It must be cold for her in that room. No fire or anything.'

She smiled. 'That is the general idea—remember? She only has a thin nightgown and no slippers. That will keep her in the blankets.'

'Still . . .' he said. 'It's nearly ready.' He turned up the gas jet. When the first bubble appeared on the milk he filled the mug.

Myra lifted the tray, and preceded by her husband went slowly upstairs. Bill unlocked the bedroom door and after holding it just wide enough for her to pass inside, closed it again quickly.

Myra stood for a moment and blinked through the yellowy fog-like gloom at the bed. The child was sitting up, propped against a pillow, holding the bedding beneath her chin. Their eyes met, and Myra smiled as she crossed the room; the girl's face remained solemn.

Myra put the tray on the bedside table, and said, 'Well, good morning, Adriana.'

The child asked, sulkily, 'Who are you? Where's my nanny?'

'All in good time, my dear.'

'And where's my daddy?'

Myra sat on the edge of the bed. She could see that the girl's eyes were puffy and red. She said, 'You have been crying.'

'No I haven't. Where's my daddy? Who are you? I don't like you.'

'Do you want some nice scrambled eggs and hot milk?'

'No.'

Myra frowned, nonplussed. She'd had little to do with children, and didn't really like them; she lacked the necessary patience to wade through their tantrums and foolishness, and could never understand why they acted so childishly. She said, 'If you do not eat this you will go hungry all day.'

'Good.'

Myra was at a loss. She searched her mind for something else to say.

Adriana said, 'If you go and fetch my daddy I'll eat my breakfast.'

Myra picked up the tray and settled it on the girl's knees. She said, 'Eat first.'

It looked for a moment as though Adriana would refuse, but then her eyes turned greedily on the food and she lifted the fork, quickly, and began to shovel the eggs into her mouth.

Myra moved back to the foot of the bed and watched in silence. When the child had emptied the dish—leaving the bread untouched—and was drinking the milk, Myra said, 'I suppose you know you are in a hospital.'

Adriana brightened. 'Am I?'

'Yes. It is for infectious complaints. That means the thing you have is catching. That is why you have a room all to yourself.'

'What've I got?'

'German measles.'

'Had it.'

'This is a special type. Double German measles.'

Adriana smiled. 'Is it very special?'

'Very. That is why we must keep it almost dark in here. And you will have to stay in bed and be very quiet. You will be here for three days, then, if you have been a good little girl and very, very quiet, you can go home.'

'And will my daddy bring me choclits and grapes and things?'

'Finish your milk.'

Adriana drained the glass, and wiped the back of her hand across her mouth. Myra said, 'All the little girls who come in here have funny dreams when they are taken sick. The girl in the room next door says she dreamt she left school and was carried away on a big white horse.'

'I have lovely dreams. Shall I tell you the one I had last night?'

'No, tell me the one you had when you were taken sick, when you left school.'

Adriana frowned, then nodded. 'Oh yes. There was a man. And we went to a field. And there was a wooden house and a motor-bike thing. And he wanted me to blow my nose. And that's all. But it wasn't a dream.'

'Was the man big and fat?'

'Oh yes, very big. Ever so big.'

'And fat.'

'Yes, ever so fat. Oh, and his hair was all shiny.'

'Black and shiny.'

'Yes.'

'A big fat man with black hair.'

'Yes.'

Myra nodded, satisfied. She said, 'Well now, tell me about your house and your own little room.'

Adriana folded her arms in a businesslike way, and began to talk. She described her house, room, toys, nanny, friends, holidays and last Christmas, all in a way that the listener could only assume must be hyperbolical. But Myra learned the names of Adriana's friends and favourite toys, which had to be facts regardless.

Finally Myra broke into the flow of talk. She'd given and taken all she wanted, and now she was bored with the child;

also the gloom was making her eyes ache. She rose and lifted the tray, and, remembering something else, asked, 'Did you see anyone in here earlier this morning?'

'Yes, a man.'

'What did he look like?'

Adriana frowned, and closed one eye thoughtfully.

Myra said quickly, 'It does not matter. It is not important.'

'You talk funny.'

'What?'

'You talk funny.'

Myra moved away, then stopped and turned, smiling. 'That is because I am a foreigner. French. But that is a secret. Promise never to tell anyone?'

'Oh I do, I promise,' said Adriana, smiling brightly. 'I hope I may die and be torn to pieces by wild dogs if I ever tell a living soul.'

Myra went to the door, opened it and slid the tray on to the landing. She straightened and turned. 'Now, you lie still like a good little girl. I shall return later.'

'When will my daddy get here?'

'Your father will not be coming. There are to be no visitors.'

Adriana bounded up and leapt to the foot of the bed. She said, loudly, 'You told me you'd fetch him if I ate my breakfast.'

'If you are nice and quiet you can go home in three days.'

Adriana shouted, 'You said you'd fetch him. You told a lie.'

'Be quiet.'

'You're a liar. You're an old cow. I hate you.' She stiffened her arms at her sides, threw back her head and began to wail loudly.

Myra reached the bed in three long strides, swung her arm and slapped the child across the face.

The wailing stopped as Adriana fell over on to her back. She lay still, her mouth open, staring with astonishment at the ceiling.

Myra grabbed her and bundled her quickly under the blankets, and said, holding her firmly by the shoulders. 'Every time you make a noise you will be beaten. Just remember that.'

The child glared, but said nothing.

Myra realized that the handkerchief had slipped back off her forehead, and turned swiftly away. As she crossed the room she heard Adriana say, softly, 'French, French, French.'

She went downstairs, tight-lipped with aggravation, and left the tray in the kitchen and passed through into the living-room. Bill was in his chair, reading the newspaper. He asked, 'O.K.?'

'She is a spoiled little brat,' Myra said, pulling the hanky from her head and throwing it on the table. 'A real daddy's girl.'

'Give you any trouble?'

'A bit. But I soon made her see she could not get away with it.'

'Well, poor kid's bound to feel strange, and act up a bit.'

Myra went to her chair and sat holding her hands to the fire. She said, 'I think she will be quiet enough.'

'What were you talking about?'

Myra told him what the child had said, and what she had said. Bill listened carefully, and complimented her on the way she'd installed a false description of him and had planted the French secret. They discussed these points at some length, then Myra went into the kitchen to prepare their breakfast. Bill followed and stood in the doorway.

He asked, 'When will you go to Barnet?'

'I think I had better set off as soon as we have eaten. It will take some time to get there.'

It was a long, boring journey. Myra went to the West End via the same route she'd taken to post the letter, and after having a coffee got on another Underground train. She had to change once more, and it was almost noon when she finally reached High Barnet. She found a cab, and settled back to enjoy the rarely afforded luxury of a taxi ride. She was a little sorry when they got to their destination.

The cab pulled into the kerb and stopped. There was a high wall of crinkly brick and just ahead a gate of intricately wrought iron. Myra walked to the gate and stood looking through at the tarmac drive that curved off into tall shrubs. She told herself she was quite calm. As she reached for the ring-handle a voice said, 'Yes?' and she started nervously.

Beyond the gate, standing to one side, was a heavily built policeman with a thick moustache. He moved forward. 'Was there something?'

'Yes. I would like to see Mr. Clayton.'

'Got an appointment?'

'Well, no.'

'I don't think he'll see you.'

'I think he will when he knows my business.'

'Oh. What's that?'

'It is in connexion with something that he is vitally concerned with at this moment.'

'Oh.' The policeman seemed uncertain, and looked down at the ground. 'Well, I suppose it's all right to try. Come on.' He swung the gate wide. 'I'll have to go up with you.'

They walked together along the drive. It curved left then right, then opened out into a wide circle around a dry fountain. Beyond the fountain was the house, a low neo-Tudor affair that wasn't as large as Myra had expected. The door had square imitation studs, and it opened quickly after the policeman's knock. A young girl in maid's uniform, who had obviously been doing a lot of crying, asked what it was. Myra silently held out her card. The maid took it and said please to wait, and closed the door again. The constable and Myra exchanged glances and smiles and cleared their throats, and the constable began to whistle quietly.

The door opened and the maid said, 'Mr. Clayton will see you, Mrs. Savage.'

Myra smiled again at the policeman and went in. She was led across the polished floor of a large hall that echoed their footsteps, and ushered into a study and left with the message, 'Mr. Clayton won't be a minute.'

There were six leather armchairs and several small tables. Three walls were book lined and the other held a long, latticed window, through which she caught a glimpse of the constable as he circled the fountain. Under the window was a radiator, and she went to it and turned her back and put her hands behind.

The door opened and Charles Clayton came in.

The first thing that Myra saw, or sensed, with surprise and a catch of her breath, was that Clayton was metagnomic, that he had the gift, that he possessed supra normal awareness. She warmed to him instantly, even though she knew, by the impersonal way he looked at her, that he didn't sense the same thing in her. His gift, she thought, wasn't that highly developed; and he probably didn't even know he had it.

Clayton looked to be in his mid-forties. He was only a little above average in height, but he had unusually broad shoulders and a deep chest, and his neck was thick. The large head was topped by wispy black hair that was ruffled untidily. His face was so broad that from the front the ears were all but hidden, and the wide, downturned mouth pulled thick folds in the heavy jowls.

He tugged at the lapels of his prickly tweed jacket, and said, 'I'm Charles Clayton, Mrs. Savage.'

'How do you do.'

He took a step forward. 'Mrs. Savage, I'm a very busy man at the moment, so I'd appreciate it if you'd please state your business without delay.'

Myra said, 'It is in connexion with your little girl.'

There was a brief, taut silence, during which Clayton's small dark eyes probed into Myra's. He said, 'Please sit down.'

Myra moved to the nearest armchair and lowered herself on to its cold surface. She was about to speak, but Clayton said, 'Just a moment. Would you mind if I got my wife in to hear this?'

'Not at all.'

He turned to the door, opened it and shouted, 'Rita!' He listened, and shouted again. From somewhere there came a faint answer, and a thud. He came and sat near Myra and brought out a flat and bent packet of cigarettes. 'Smoke?'

'No thank you.'

'Do you mind . . .?'

'Not at all.'

He lighted up, his movements, Myra noted with pleasure, steady and unhurried. She also noted that his left hand, which ever since he'd entered the room had been hovering around, patting, and sliding in and out of his jacket pocket, was now plunged inside the pocket firmly. She realized, with a quickening of her pulse, that the pocket probably held the ransom letter.

A tall woman came in softly and reached behind her to close the door. She was very blonde, almost white, and the hair hung loosely around her shoulders. Above her blue eyes the lids were puffy, and below them were dark shadows. She was pale, and wore only a touch of makeup, and looked young enough to be Clayton's daughter.

'My wife . . . Mrs. Savage,' said the man, without rising.

The women nodded at one another, and Mrs. Clayton moved across to an armchair. She sat down, folded her arms and looked at her feet.

In answer to a questioning look from the man, Myra said, 'Well, you may think I am wasting your time and my own in coming here, for I do not have anything concrete— concrete, that is, to you—that I can tell you. But I had to come, after I saw that piece in the paper this morning. I felt what I had to say might take some of the worry off your minds.'

'What *have* you got to say, Mrs. Savage?'

'Last night I had a dream.'

The woman looked up quickly. Clayton groaned with annoyance and rose to his feet. He said, 'Half an hour ago I had a man here who'd also read that my daughter was missing, and that I was wealthy. He offered to find her with the aid of a divining rod.'

Mrs. Clayton said, 'Please, Charlie.'

His pocket bulged as his fist clenched. He sat again, breathed deeply, swallowed and said, 'All right, Mrs. Savage. Go on.'

Myra said, 'As you saw on my card, I am a medium. My dreams are not without significance.'

Clayton blew out a stream of smoke. 'I'm afraid I'm rather a sceptic where things of that sort are concerned. To say the least.'

His wife leaned forward slightly. 'What was the dream?'

'I saw a little girl sitting alone. She was crying, and I could tell that she was lost.'

'What's the connexion with my little girl?' asked Clayton.

His wife said, 'What did she look like?'

'Well, I could not see. Her hands were covering her face. But her hair was black and straight.'

The woman nodded eagerly. Clayton said, 'Lots of children have straight black hair. Why on earth would you connect the dream with the . . . the disappearance of my child?'

'It was the symbolism. The girl was surrounded by clay,

wet clay. It was a very dominant factor in the dream. When I read that piece in this morning's paper I coupled the clay with your name.'

'Oh really now. Don't you think that's rather vague.'

'Perhaps. That is why I said I might be wasting your time and mine by coming here. But there is one way to establish for certain if the girl was yours.'

'Yes?'

'The names she used. They meant nothing to me, but they might to you.'

Mrs. Clayton asked, 'What were they?'

'First of all I heard her say Nanny, then Maureen.'

Looking at her husband, Mrs. Clayton said quickly, 'The Smiths' girl. Her name's Maureen.'

Myra went on, 'Then she said Adele.'

'That's her best friend,' gasped the woman. The man frowned.

'And just before the dream ended she said Bimbo and Peter.'

The woman jumped to her feet. 'Her toys! Those are the names of her favourite toys, the ones she sleeps with. No one could possibly know about them. No one but Adriana.'

Clayton said sharply, 'Please calm yourself.'

She sat down again, and leaned forward, her cheeks red, and fixed her eyes on the face of the visitor.

Clayton was gazing down at his smouldering cigarette. He turned aside to stub it out before saying, looking abruptly at Myra, 'As I told you before, Mrs. Savage, I don't believe in ghosts and whatnot. You could easily have learned, possibly by accident, at any time during the last year or so, the names you just mentioned; from the maids when they're out, from the cook, who always gossips in the shops, or from any of my employees. I know they're all fond of the child and talk about her. But let's put all that to one side. I would like to know just one thing. What, Mrs. Savage, do you want?'

Myra frowned, as though puzzled. 'Want?'

Clayton spread his hands, and looked from side to side across the space between them, as if something outstanding lay there. 'Obviously,' he said, 'you have a motive for coming here. You haven't travelled thirty miles for nothing.'

Myra straightened. 'My motive was compassion, and nothing else. If you are thinking I want money, you are quite wrong. I want nothing, except perhaps your thanks. I thought, on reading the paper and presuming the connexion, that I would go and tell the probably distraught parents that I knew their child to be unharmed. I thought they would be relieved to be told of my dream, and know that she was safe.'

'But,' Mr. Clayton said, 'she is not safe.'

'Oh?'

He stood up and tugged on the lapels of his jacket. 'I suppose it's all right to tell you. The story's been given to the Press, on the advice of the police. My daughter has been abducted, kidnapped, and is being held for ransom.'

Myra's hands rose quickly to knuckle her jaw. She gasped, 'Oh, how awful. I am so terribly sorry.'

Clayton nodded vaguely and walked to the door. He pulled his left hand from his pocket and let it dangle at his side, and Myra saw a knot of black hair clutched in the fingers. He opened the door. 'You'll have to excuse me, Mrs. Savage. I'm very busy. Thanks for coming.' He looked pointedly at his wife and went out.

Mrs. Clayton rose, and Myra with her. There was a brief silence, then the tall woman said, smiling, 'You've eased my mind a lot, really you have. You didn't waste your journey.'

'I am so glad. And I feel sure your little girl will be quite all right.'

'Thank you.'

Mrs. Clayton led the way into the hall, and as they crossed it said, 'I would like to . . . give you, at least, your expenses.'

'That is kind of you, but I really could not accept it.'

The blonde woman opened the front door and held out her hand. Myra took it, saying, 'Do not hesitate to come and see me if you feel the need.'

'Thank you.'

Myra went outside and set off briskly across the tarmac circle. She was pleased with herself. The interview had gone more or less as she'd expected, and had accomplished its purpose. She had introduced herself into the affair, made herself known, and that was all that was necessary for the moment. Even though the supranormal element was not accepted by Clayton, the idea of it had been implanted, and, she knew, was already fully believed by the wife. But that didn't count for much, she thought; Clayton was the boss.

She approached the gate. The policeman was leaning against the wall at the side, smoking. He heard her footsteps and quickly dropped the cigarette and stepped forward. Touching his helmet, he asked, 'All finished, ma'am?'

'Yes, thank you.'

'I—er—forgot to ask you when you went in, but could I have your name and address, please? I'm supposed to take the names of all people coming and going.'

Myra gave him one of her cards. He read it, nodding slowly, put it away and pulled open the gate. As she passed through Myra noticed a car standing across the street; several men were sitting inside it, all looking at her. The policeman whispered, 'Reporters.'

'Of course,' Myra said. 'Well, good afternoon.' She walked away, not too quickly, and glanced back at the car and wished the reporters would come after her and ask a few questions. She could just let it slip out, the purpose of her visit. But they only stared. It did not matter, she thought; there was plenty of time later for publicity.

She started walking faster, heading for the centre of town, and decided that since the trip had gone so well she would splurge and take a taxi all the way home.

Bill helped his wife off with her coat, folded it neatly and draped it on the banister. He said, 'The kettle's on. We'll have a nice cuppa in a minute.'

They went into the lounge and sat before the fire. Myra relived the interview with the Claytons, as close to word-for-word as she could remember, starting and ending with the constable. Bill was an appreciative audience; not only because he was interested and concerned, but also because his wife was expending all her talk on him, and only him. One slightly unpleasant thing in the story was when she mentioned, eagerly, that Clayton had extra-sensory gifts; Bill always felt his lack painfully, and suffered a pang of jealousy and envy.

After the tea was brewed and they were each holding a cup and saucer on their knees, Myra asked, 'How did things go here?'

Bill shook his head. 'She kicked up a heck of a fuss.'

'Oh?'

'It was after dinner. I made her a cheese and tomato sandwich and cocoa. I just slid the tray inside the door, quick like.'

'What did she do?'

'Oh, she screamed and carried on, and I'm sure I heard some crockery break. She banged and banged on the door. And the names she used; you'd wonder where a little girl learned them.'

'Expensive schools. That is where they use the filthiest language.'

'Well, it wasn't filthy. Just bitch and cow-face and pig. But the noise she made. It was terrible. I slipped out into the back garden, and d'you know, I could hear her, even through the plywood.'

Myra lifted her eyebrows. 'But when we tested it, when you shouted in the bedroom, I could not hear anything outside.'

'Yes, I know. What a pair of lungs. And after that she sang "Onward Christian Soldiers" four times. I thought she'd never stop.'

Tapping a foot with annoyance, Myra said, 'The spoiled brat. We need not have gone to all that trouble with the hospital story, painting the things white and so on. We should have put up more plywood instead.'

They finished their tea in silence. Myra put her cup on the mantel and rose. 'I suppose I had better go up and see what damage she has done.'

Bill said, 'I'll warm the tea, and you can take her some.'

Myra took her coat upstairs, and paused outside the back bedroom; she could hear nothing. After slipping on the white dress she went back down to the lounge to get the handkerchief. Above the sideboard was a mirror with a crudely painted crinolined lady in one corner. Myra carefully arranged the handkerchief over her hair, keeping the front low on her brow.

Bill came in from the kitchen, carrying a cup and saucer and a plate holding a slab of cake. Myra took them from him, saying, 'She does not really deserve this.'

They went into the hall. Bill was on the fourth step and Myra on the bottom one when they heard the squeal of a car's brakes. They both froze. A car door banged. Bill turned and looked at his wife. She frowned him into silence.

There was the sound of footsteps, and a dark shape grew on the glass of the front door. The top of the shape came to a point.

Both Myra and Bill had the same thought—*police*—and their hearts began to beat faster. They exchanged a swift wide-eyed glance before fixing their gaze on the door.

The arm of the shape moved, and the tiny knocker above the keyhole was rattled viciously. The sound, though expected, made Bill jump, and he jumped again when another shape suddenly appeared on the glass. This one had no point, and he thought: *detective*.

There was a cough from outside, and a muffled voice said, 'Try again, Sergeant.' Once more the knocker was rattled, and a fist rapped hard on the glass.

Myra's arms began to ache from holding the crockery, and her fingers were paining from their tautness. Suddenly her nose started to itch, and she opened her mouth and flared her nostrils tightly.

The flat-topped shape moved out of sight, going to the left. Bill set a foot slowly, quietly and gently on to the step below and, ignoring his wife's glare, put one hand on the banister, one on the wall and lowered his head close to hers. He whispered, 'He'll see the fire. He'll know we're home.'

She looked quickly at the closed door of the front room. Her nose stopped itching and her face relaxed, and she hissed, all but inaudibly, 'No. Your chair hides it from the window.'

'The glow. He'll see that.'

'No. It was just smouldering.'

Bill nodded, and blew out softly through pursed lips. But almost at once he got another chilling thought. He whispered, 'They'll see the smoke from the chimney.'

Myra lifted her eyes to the ceiling, and shrugged. 'It does not have to mean we are in. Anyway, there is nothing we can do about it.'

'Perhaps they won't look.'

The missing shape came back, moved across to the right and disappeared again. The other shape went after it. From the attached garage came the sound of wood knocking on wood.

Bill hissed, 'They're trying the garage door.'

'Is it locked?'

'Yes.'

'Can they see in?'

He shook his head, listening hard. He heard faint footsteps coming from beyond the side of the house, and said, 'They must be going to look round the back. They might try the door.'

'Is it locked?'

'No,' he said, and added, almost as though he were asking a question, 'But they wouldn't dare come in.'

A noise came from above; it sounded like a plate being smashed. They both jerked their heads up. Bill's stiffened arms began to tremble. He dropped them from the banister and wall and sat down, closing his eyes. He mumbled, 'If they hear her . . .'

Myra crossed quickly to the shallow hat-stand that was spreadeagled against the wall, and slid the crockery on to its small shelf, then clasped her hands together, massaging away the stiffness, and relieving her fear and tension by being able to perform the action.

There was another noise from upstairs; a dull thud. Bill kept his eyes closed. He was badly frightened.

Myra backed away from the hat-stand to the wall opposite, and sat shakily on the slim wooden cupboard that hid the gas-meter. She knew now that the private theory she had held was right. It was natural that as soon as she introduced herself into the affair she would be suspect. She hadn't voiced this to Bill; the pros of the Plan weren't strong enough to stand too many cons. There was grave danger ahead, she thought.

Changes would have to be made . . . if they were free to make them.

A fist pounded heavily on the back door, making an ominous booming sound that reverberated around the kitchen. Myra held her breath and looked up toward the head of the stairs, her hands clinging tightly to one another.

Bill waited for the next noise to come from above, and prayed it wouldn't. His heart seemed to be striking against the side of his breastbone; striking loud enough for him to hear. He put his hand to his chest, and through the jacket, sweater, shirt, vest and chest-protector he could feel the beat.

The silence, oppressive and painful, went on. Then, faintly at first, but getting quickly louder, the footsteps started again. They grew, scuffling, without rhythm, to a loud pound, and faded rapidly away. Another moment of silence before a car door, two doors, slammed.

Bill drew a long breath, and Myra let one out, and they exchanged looks of unhappy, face-sagging exhaustion. They listened listlessly to the car start, rev up, whine away and fade from earshot.

Myra leaned her head back on the wall and looked at the cobweb in the corner above the hat-stand. She said, tiredly, 'Of course, I realize now it was to be expected, that I would come under suspicion, knowing so much about the child.'

'Maybe they wanted something else.'

'No,' she said, shaking her head. 'They think it possible that we have the child. That is quite natural. And of course they have to check.'

'I suppose so.' Bill thought for a moment before saying, 'They'll be back then.'

'Sure to be.'

He put a ringer inside his collar and ran it around from left to right, and wiped the moisture off on to his sleeve. He cleared his throat, and asked, 'What do we do now?'

Myra sighed and pushed herself erect. 'Change the plans . . . slightly. But first of all I will see to the child. You go and lock the back door.' She collected the crockery off the hat-stand shelf, and handed the cup and saucer to her husband as he came off the bottom step. 'Take that with you.'

'I could warm it,' he said, without enthusiasm.

'Never mind.' She went upstairs, unlocked the bedroom and went in.

Adriana jerked up into a sitting position, and immediately bounced back flat again and covered her head with the blankets. Myra looked around the floor. The tray was under the bed, and scattered across the carpet were fragments of china; but there was no food to be seen. Had Myra seen this before the police visit she would have been furious, but now she hadn't the energy for any emotion, other than worry.

She retrieved the tray and put the plate on it, leaving the slice of cake only on the bedside table, and collected the bits and pieces off the floor, ignoring the smaller chips.

Back in the lounge, she said, absently, 'What a mess,' and put the tray on the table. Taking a dining-chair across the room she set it with its back to the writing desk. She sat down and looked out of the window, and had a clear view of the whole street right up to the corner.

Bill, standing on the hearth rug, cleared his throat and said, 'Look, I've been thinking about it. Wouldn't it be just the same if I took her tonight to that shed, and left her there, and then you phone the Claytons, or the newspapers, which-ever you think best? Wouldn't it be just the same?'

'Hardly. The story would be over before it has started. It has to have a build-up of several days in the papers—or, I should say, it would be better to have. I am afraid it will be necessary now to cut it short. But not too short.'

'You mean, still get the money and so on.'

'Of course. That is the part that will make it a big story. Such things are extremely rare. And after we have come this far it would be ridiculous to throw that part of the scheme away.'

'But we can't keep her here. They'll be back if they think we've got her.' He blinked rapidly. 'Maybe at any minute.'

Irritably, Myra said, 'They do not think we have got her. Nobody said that. It is simply a possibility that they have to check. Just the normal routine of investigation. If they had a strong suspicion they would not have left.'

'But they will be back. You said so.'

'Yes.' She glanced up the street. 'But perhaps not tonight. And if they do, we shall do the same as we did before. Also we will let the fire go out and not put any lights on after. Tomor-row you will take the child with you.'

'Where to?'

'Nowhere. Just with you, when you go to collect the money.'

'Oh.'

'Tonight, as soon as it is dark, you will go over the fields, the back way, and get to the centre of the city. Just make the phone call as we planned, arranging to meet Clayton tomorrow.'

Bill licked his lips, thoroughly, and said nothing.

Myra went on, 'In the morning you, and the girl, will be away for several hours, and during that time the police will come back and I shall show them around the house, even if they have not got a search warrant. When you return you simply bring the child in again. Then the next day we arrange for her to be found. We do everything, in fact, that we planned to, except that we reduce the time by two or three days.'

Bill said, 'Why can't we arrange for her to be found the same day?'

'There would not be time for the story of the money to be widely reported.'

'And what if the police haven't been here by the time I get back?'

Myra looked back at the street. 'Yes, that is right.' After a pause, she said, 'We will arrange a signal. I will hang a bed-sheet on the washing line and leave it there till the police have been and gone, then take it down. Before you come home, drive to one of those streets at the edge of the estate. If the sheet is still up, keep driving around, coming back at regular intervals to check.'

Bill nodded. After a moment he said, 'Do you think they might be watching the house? Is that why you said I should go the back way?'

'I think it is a possibility. One we can not afford to over-look.'

They were sitting side by side on the bottom step of the stair-case, their eyes on the door. It was dusk now, and it was cold. Myra was wearing her overcoat, and Bill his raincoat and scarf.

There came the familiar sound of a whistled tune, and they both tensed. A moment later there was a clang as the paper boy's bicycle was let fall against the wall. A short blur appeared on the glass, and the newspaper thudded half-way through the slot.

When the boy's whistle had died away, Bill went to the door and bent down. He paused, and looked back at his wife. 'You don't suppose they'll be watching very close and see me pull the paper in?'

She shook her head. 'Anyway, the wall hides it.'

He jerked the paper through quickly, and flapped it out of its folds as he straightened. His wife came to his side and they stood with their backs to the door to get the benefit of the light, and looked at the front page. The main headline was political. To one side of it and slightly below was the heading *Abduction in Barnet*. Underneath was a blurred photo of a girl's face.

Myra said, 'Look for the personal column first.'

Bill turned the pages to the classified advertisements. They saw at once the item that concerned them; it was at the head of the column. It said, *Longfellow. Am ready to oblige. Charles.*

Peering close, they read the item through several times before Bill turned back to the front page. Myra said, 'You read it out. The poor light hurts my eyes.' She returned to the stairs and sat down.

Bill cleared his throat, and read: '*It was officially announced today by Mr. Charles Clayton of* . . . et cetera . . . um . . . *that his only child, Adriana, aged six, a pupil at* . . . um . . . *was abducted from outside the school yesterday afternoon as she was leaving for home. It is believed she is being held for ransom. The Clayton chauffeur, Henry Webster, aged forty-six, said that he called for the child as usual and put her in the back of the car. A stranger approached him and said the principal had a letter for Mr. Clayton. The chauffeur went into the school. He returned a minute later and found that the car and child were gone. The car, a black Bentley saloon, has not yet been found. The stranger is described as being of medium height, middle-age, and with black hair and the features of a boxer. Police are anxious to interview the owner of a green van which was seen in the vicinity of the school before and after the abduction. The mother of the girl was the former* . . . er . . . *Adriana is described as being small for her age. She has black hair with a fringe. Four upper front teeth are missing. When last seen she was wearing a green beret, green coat and brown stockings.*' He lowered the paper and looked at his wife.

She asked, 'Is that all?'

'Yes. Not much, is it?'

'Just the bare details. It was, after all, given to the papers at short notice. There will be more later.'

'It doesn't mention the ransom letter.'

'No. I think Clayton will keep quiet about that till after, after he has paid. He will not wish to endanger the child's life, as per the threat in the letter.'

Bill said, frowning at the ceiling, 'I wonder if they're planning to try and catch the man who'll collect the money.'

'Hardly. I am sure Clayton would not stand for that. He thinks more of his child than he does of the money. In any case, they would be unsuccessful, the way you have it planned.'

Bill looked at the paper again and read the description of himself. It rather pleased him. He said, 'D'you think anyone would recognize me from this?'

'Not a hope.' She glanced at the feeble light behind the glass of the door. 'It will be dark soon. We will wait another ten minutes.'

They waited twenty minutes, to be sure. They sat on the stairs, huddled together for warmth, and talked in low voices. When the hat-stand became merely a black patch, Myra said, 'All right.' They rose and fumbled their way into the kitchen.

Bill unlocked the door and slipped out, and Myra put her head out beside him. They listened. All was quiet.

She hissed, 'Think you will be able to see?'

'Yes.'

'You know what to say?'

He patted his pocket. 'I've got it all written down.'

'Right. I will wait up for you.' She withdrew her head and closed the door softly.

Bill began to move slowly forward along the earth path that stood out vaguely from its surrounds. It was a moonless night, and there were few stars. On his left and ahead was only blackness, with nothing to show the division of earth and sky. Over to the right was a scattering of lighted windows, and above them rooftops were faintly silhouetted against the pale glow of street lamps.

The path ended, and he was by the rotting fence that separated his garden from the wasteland. By bending down and peering he found a place where several pales had fallen away, and he put his fingertips to the ground to crawl through. He straightened and began to edge slowly over the lumpy ground, his hands held in front, trying to avoid stumbling, but stumbling anyway, on the closely set, dense tufts of grass, heading straight forward into the darkness. He knew it would be far simpler to follow the fence, backing as it did the other gardens, but he might be seen, and assumed to be up to no good, lurking quietly in the dark, and be the object of a phone call to the police.

He put thirty slowly covered yards between himself and his house before turning right and heading for the lighted windows. As he drew closer he made an open street-end his goal, and began to move faster. He was pleased with himself for managing so well, and the depression that had come with the police visit lifted a little.

He was within a stone's throw of his goal when a car suddenly swung into the well-lit street and came racing down toward him.

Almost before he'd told himself to drop flat, he'd done it. His stomach and elbows hit the ground with a painful thud.

The car's headlights whited the air above him, and he clung close to the ground, grabbing grass in either hand. He could feel a pulse beating strongly under his Adam's apple; but he felt drearily unhappy more than frightened.

There was a squeal of brakes, followed by silence. A moment later the headlights went out. He waited for the sound of opening doors. When none came he slowly lifted his head. The car was close, its front wheels standing on the edge of the tarmac, and inside were the silhouettes of two people.

Only when he lowered his head did he realize it was possible the car had no connexion at all with the police. It was just his guilt that made him assume it had. He spent five minutes debating whether or not the police would park right there and if they'd put their lights off. He looked up again, and saw that the two heads in the car were welded together, and that one was definitely female.

He rose to his feet, grinning with rue, and brushed himself off. His knees felt damp, and he told himself he was in for it if he didn't remember to give them a good rub with embrocation.

He reached the roadway and passed the car, and its occupants didn't move a fraction out of their clinch. Walking smartly he came to the end of the street, and went along another identical with it. He turned on to a main road and headed for a bench where several people were standing. A bus roared by him to pull up squealing at the bench, and he had to run to get it. He went upstairs and darted a quick look around the other half dozen passengers; but none of them were known to him. At the eighth stop he got off, in a small shopping district, and walked around a corner to a shelter, where he stood and waited, turning his back to the two women also waiting. A trolley-bus came and he boarded it, and fifteen minutes later arrived at a tube station.

In the station he stopped long enough to buy an evening paper, different from the one delivered to the house, and quickly got his ticket and went to the platform. In this newspaper the abduction had displaced the political news, and the picture of the girl was twice as large, but the story was almost identical with the other. Bill supposed it must have been given to the Press in the form of a written statement. He re-read the description of himself, then, when he thought he was unobserved, dropped the paper on to the tracks.

A train came. He got in and sat at one end, where he faced only an empty seat and a wall of wood. Usually the warm compartments of the Underground cheered him, but now he was unaffected. He brought a piece of paper from his pocket and read the long-hand on it, practising what he would say to Charles Clayton on the telephone, mumbling to himself and timing the speech with his wrist-watch. He thought it would be easily short enough to eliminate the danger of the call being traced.

At the Bank he changed to the Northern Line. When the train drew in at the Elephant and Castle he joined up with a small group of people who had also left the train and stayed with them till he was out of the station. He began to walk quickly along a main road. The district was unknown to him, but to him this was unimportant. He passed one empty telephone kiosk, thinking it best to put a little distance between himself and the station, and stopped at another farther along. He put a handful of change on the shelf and, using a handkerchief, lifted the receiver. The number he knew by heart. He put coins in the slot and dialled.

His call was answered so quickly that it startled him. A voice said, 'Yes? Charles Clayton here.'

Bill, speaking from the back of his throat, said, 'This is Longfellow.'

There was a sound that might have been a gasp, then, 'Where's my little girl? What have you done with her?' The voice was steady to start with, but on the last words it trembled and rose to a higher key.

Bill closed his eyes, wilting at the anguish that came over the wires. He would have given anything to be able to tell the man that the child was well and not to worry. But he couldn't do that.

He asked, as sternly as he could, 'You want her back, don't you?'

A pause, pregnant in its silence, then, hoarsely, 'Yes.'

'Have you got the money ready?'

'Yes.'

'In the bag with the B.O.A.C. initials?'

'Yes.'

'Then listen carefully. Tomorrow morning come into town. Carry the bag openly, not wrapped. Just before twelve o'clock noon go into Leicester Square. In the top left corner—the north-west corner—of the inside part of the square, you'll find a row of telephone booths. The last one on the row, the last one west, is the one you want. Go inside it at twelve o'clock and wait there. Don't do anything, don't use the phone, just wait there. Got all that?'

'Yes.'

'North-west corner, last booth west. And listen, if there's any cops with you, you'll be sorry. Understand?'

'Yes.'

'Good night.'

'Wait,' the voice said quickly, 'I want . . .'

Bill lowered the receiver and set it back in its cradle. He took the change off the shelf and put it in his pocket, and wiped the shelf with his handkerchief. Leaning his back against the door he pushed his way out, and used the handkerchief again on the outside handle.

He began to walk briskly, away from the station. He'd just decided not to go back by the same route; it was possible that someone could have noticed him leave the station, and see him return five minutes later. He would cross the river and get the tube from there.

The street was brightly lit, from both lamps and shop windows, but there were few people about. He signalled to the first taxi that came along. It was engaged, and so were the next two. He felt a slight panic, and walked faster, and glanced back at the telephone kiosk.

Then a vacant cab came from the other direction, and at his whistle swung across the road. He jumped in and said, 'St. Paul's.'

Three

IT WAS STILL DARK when Myra got up. She had told herself repeatedly the night before that she must not sleep later than five o'clock, and it was at five exactly that she awoke. She dressed quickly, adding the white frock—glad of it now for the extra warmth—and the white head covering, and went in to rouse the child.

Adriana was cross at being dragged from warm sleep, and grumbled, even though told it was midday, and tried to hide under the bedding and get back to sleep again. But she was made to sit up and stay awake.

Myra spent the next two hours in her own room, a blanket around her, but going at regular intervals to look in on the child; she wanted her awake now and tired later.

At seven o'clock she went down to the lounge. Giving her husband a shake, she said, 'Come on. There is a lot to do.' He nodded, blinking, and began to get up. She hurried him along. When he was almost finished dressing she went back upstairs, wrapped the girl in a blanket and carried her into the bathroom.

After having a brief wash in the kitchen, Bill got a screwdriver and went up to the back bedroom. The plywood was fitted right inside the frame of the window and held by eight screws. He removed it swiftly and lowered it to the floor. The table and chair were taken aside and the carpet pulled from under the head legs of the bed and rolled down to the feet. He slid the sheet of plywood beneath the bed, and when the carpet was rolled back over it the ridge it made was negligible, and unseen anyway from a standing position. He replaced the table and chair, switched off the light and opened the window, and was finished. He tapped on the bathroom door and went downstairs.

Myra had supervised the child's toilet and was now combing her hair. Adriana had proved tiredly malleable, standing meekly with one foot on top of the other, and now, when Myra said, 'Sit on the stool,' she sat.

Myra opened the medicine cabinet and brought out the bottle of chloroform. With her back to the girl she poured a little of the fluid on a corner of the towel, and turned. 'Close your eyes a moment.' Adriana's eyelids sank. Myra put the towel gently to the girl's face, and with the other hand held her firmly by the shoulders. She said, 'Breathe deeply.'

Bill had put on his coat, scarf, helmet and goggles, and was pulling on his gloves as he walked down the hall. He opened the front door and stepped outside, and began to stretch his arms in an imitation yawn, his head moving around slowly.

He was thankful to see that there were no signs of life anywhere.

Unlocking the garage he swung open the right-hand half of the door, and left it at an angle to the house, where it screened off the garage and the side path from the rest of the street. After starting the motor-cycle engine and laying the side-car cover right back he walked round to the back and in by the kitchen door.

On the table was a carrier bag, a blue cap, and a blue plastic pack the size and shape of a small book. The carrier bag he folded and slid inside the breast of his coat, and the cap and pack he put in his pockets.

He went into the hall just as his wife was coming down the stairs. Myra had the blanket-swathed child in her arms and was clutching the chloroform bottle in one hand.

Bill asked, 'Is she away?'

'Yes. Sound as a bell.'

'How much did you give her?'

'I simply poured a drop on the towel. I know as little about it as you do.'

He held out his arms as she reached the bottom step, but she said, 'I might as well take her. Get the bottle.'

He took the chloroform and led the way to the kitchen, and outside and round to the front. In the garage Myra put the girl into the side-car and stretched her out full-length. Bill tested the cork of the bottle before wedging it safely in a pocket of the side-car. He pulled the waterproof tight and snapped it down.

Myra asked, 'You have got everything?'

'Yes. You can manage the bathroom?'

'Yes. You will not forget the fruit?'

'No. And you won't forget the sheet?'

'No. I will do it now.'

'Right.' He swung on to the saddle, tucked his coat tails under him and gently opened the throttle.

Myra went outside, looked up the street, and glanced back and nodded.

Bill moved the machine forward and steered it slowly out and eased it down on to the dirt road. He pulled the goggles over his eyes and set off, keeping the speed down so there would be no bouncing.

Myra closed and locked the garage and went back inside the house, going straight up to the bathroom. The sheet of plywood was smaller than the other and was not screwed in, merely wedged against the frame—it hadn't to withstand any possible batterings. She took it down and carried it to the bed in the back room. With some difficulty she slid it under the mattress, well under, and put the bedding back in its previous disorder. She examined the pillow closely, and found three long black hairs, which she carried to the window and blew outside. Downstairs again she folded the blankets on the couch, leaving aside a sheet, ready to be taken to the washing line.

Bill came out of the housing estate and turned on to the main road. The traffic was light and fast. He steered in close to the kerb and drove along beside it, the side-car wheel almost in the gutter, driving at a steady twenty. He had a lot of time to spend, and he hoped the lack of speed would help grade the girl's artificial sleep into a natural one.

After travelling five miles he came to a gentle stop in front of a transport café, into which, with several bikeward glances, he went. He never felt quite real till he'd had his morning tea, and he needed it now more than usual.

He'd passed the café a thousand times, but this was the first time he'd been inside. It was small and dirty, not a bit like its gaudily painted exterior. There were no other customers; but two cats were asleep in the centre of one of the tables. Behind the counter was a heavy-eyed youth, who said, as Bill approached, 'Cook's not'ere yet, if you wanted breakfast.'

'No. Just tea, please.'

'Right you are.'

Bill put the money on the counter, and asked, 'Have you got the morning paper?'

The youth, busy at the tea urn, nodded his head to the side. 'On the chair there.'

At the end of the counter was a backless chair holding a pile of newspapers. Bill picked up the top one, his eyes full of the blaring headline KIDNAPPING IN BARNET and the four-inch-square picture of Adriana, and tucked it casually under his arm.

Taking his tea to a window table, he sat down facing his machine, and gave it a glance before turning to the paper. The photo of Adriana was different from the one used the day before; it was clear and recent, though not too recent—the smile showed a full row of upper teeth. The story was longer, but substantially the same. The Bentley had been found, and was being checked for fingerprints, as was the cricket pavilion, inside and out. There was no mention of the green van, whose driver the police had wished to interview, but now a small car of the eight, or less, horse-power class was being sought.

Bill frowned thoughtfully at this last piece of information, puzzled by the fact that it said only that the car was small, without giving type or colour, and realized slowly, with a happy lift of his eyebrows, that the tracks left in the field by his machine had been assumed to be those of a small car. Which assumption, he thought, was perfectly natural; no one would ever dream of a motor-bike being used in an abduction.

He was quite cheered by this development, and, without thinking, turned to the youth and said, 'How about this kidnapping in Barnet?' Then he blinked, shocked and surprised at his own audacity, and turned away with a jerk.

He heard the youth give a non-committal grunt, and say, 'I like the look of Preston North End, don't you?'

Bill said, 'Ah.' He drank his tea hurriedly, and sidled out with his back to the counter.

The police came at ten o'clock. Myra was ready for them, and quite calm. Wearing an apron and a dustcap she walked slowly to the front door and opened it. There were two of them, one in uniform.

The plain-clothes man looked to be close to retirement, and was very nearly fat. Hatless, his white hair a glistening contrast to his plump red face, he seemed to Myra to be anything but a policeman. He asked, smiling pleasantly, 'Mrs. Savage?'

'I am she.'

He brought a card from his macintosh pocket and held it in front of her eyes. 'I'm a police officer. Detective Sergeant Beedle. From the local station.'

'Oh. How do you do.'

'How do you do. I'd like a word or two with you, Mrs. Savage, if it's no inconvenience.'

'Why yes,' Myra said, in a faintly surprised tone. 'Of course. Will you come in?'

The detective turned to the uniformed man. 'I think you can wait, Sergeant.' He followed Myra into the lounge, and said, 'We called yesterday afternoon, but you were out.'

'Oh yes. Walking.' She indicated the couch, and sat down herself at the table, pulling the cap from her head. She asked, 'It is not about the radio licence, is it?'

He laughed, lowering himself slowly on to the couch. 'No, nothing like that. It's nothing at all, really. Just a check. It's in connexion with the little girl who's missing in Barnet.'

'Ah, of course.'

'I believe you called on the Claytons?'

'Yes. It was because of a dream I had had.' She told him, briefly, the story of the dream.

He nodded, and, smiling shyly, said, 'I think you know my wife, by the way. She's been to one or two of your séances. Millie Beedle. We live in Bar Grove.'

Myra did vaguely recall the name, but nothing else. She said, 'Oh, so you are Mrs. Beedle's husband. A charming woman. I do not think she mentioned that she was married to a policeman.'

He winked. 'Probably ashamed of it.'

Myra smiled. Beedle laughed, heartily. When his face straightened, he said, 'Well, now to business. It's like this you see. After your visit to Barnet yesterday, the police there called us and asked if we'd check on you, character and so on. I was able to tell them at once that you weren't known, officially, to us, and had an exemplary character. That was all right, but they asked if we'd have a look over the house.'

'The house?' Myra said, with a puzzled frown.

'Yes. You see, in cases of this type we can't afford to over-look any possibility, no matter how remote.'

'Naturally. But what has the house to do with it?'

'Well,' he said, grinning. 'You could have the Clayton child hidden away here for all we know.'

She also grinned. 'Oh, I see.' She was getting a little tired of his almost permanent amusement, and wondered if it could be merely an act to put her off guard.

Serious again, he said, 'So I'd like to have a look around. Just a formality. There's no search warrant, so of course you're perfectly at liberty to refuse.'

Myra rose. 'I should not dream of refusing, naturally. I am more than willing to co-operate. Where shall we start?'

The plump detective sighed to his feet. 'Well, let's just have a quick peep at this part of the house, then go upstairs.'

They went into the kitchen, and Beedle glanced around, nodding, and poked his head into the pantry. As they passed through into the hall he asked, 'Is your husband at home?'

'No. He went out for a bit of fresh air.'

'He isn't working in this area, is he?'

'No, he is not working at all. He suffers with ill-health.'

Beedle looked in the cluttered cupboard under the stairs. 'Oh yes, I think I remember my wife mentioning something about it. Asthma, isn't it?'

'Yes. Chronic.'

They went upstairs, the policeman slowly, and entered the back bedroom. Myra bustled housewifely over to the bed and began to straighten the blankets. 'Dear me, what a mess.'

He laughed. 'Oh, don't worry about that.' His eyes skipped idly over the meagre furnishings and the upside-down carpet, and he asked, 'This is your room?'

'No, my husband's. I keep it bare and dust free. For his chest, you know.'

He nodded, and swung about casually and strolled into the bathroom. Myra followed and stood in the doorway. After examining the insides of the large airing cupboard, Beedle fixed his gaze on the ceiling. Myra looked up. There was a small trap door.

She asked, 'Do you want to go up there? I have step-ladders downstairs.'

He turned and looked at her, smiling broadly. 'I don't think the Clayton girl's up there, do you?'

Myra could see that although his smile was real enough, his eyes were barely affected by it and were watching her face closely. She said coyly, 'Well, you never can tell.'

He laughed, and dismissed the trap door with a shrug.

She took him to the box-room, and he showed surprise at the crammed furniture. She explained, as she led the way into the séance room, 'The wardrobe and dresser are usually kept in here, but we move them out when there is to be a séance, as there is tonight.'

His interest now, as he looked at the table and row of chairs, was, Myra felt, quite unofficial. She said, 'It is a terrible thing, is it not, this kidnapping.'

He nodded solemnly. 'It certainly is. Thank heavens they're not common.'

'Have there been any new developments?'

'Well, of course, I don't know much about the case myself. But there's one new thing I heard this morning. It seems they aren't too happy with the chauffeur. That's strictly between you and me, by the way. Though I dare say it'll come out pretty soon.'

'You mean the Claytons' chauffeur?'

'Yes. Seems he has a record. Some sort of robbery about twenty years ago. Served six months for it.'

'Oh dear. That does not look very good, does it?'

'No indeed. But the main thing is, his story of what happened is a bit thin.'

'What happened when the child was taken?'

'Yes.'

'I read in the paper that a stranger told him to go in the school and get a letter, and he did, and when he came out the car was gone. Was that untrue?'

'Well, that's his story. He says he went in the school and asked someone the way to the principal's office, but then he got confused and didn't find it and came outside again. He says he saw the car wasn't there, and didn't know what to think, so he set off to walk home.'

'That was rather stupid.'

'Yes. It's that, the long delay in reporting the car miss-ing, that our people weren't happy with. Then they couldn't find the person the chauffeur said he'd asked directions from in the school. And they couldn't find anyone who'd seen the stranger take the car away, or even seen the chauf-feur walking.'

'Funny.'

'Very.'

Myra sighed and said, 'I do so hope the poor child will be found quickly. Her parents are worried to death.'

'Oh, I dare say it'll be soon cleared up.'

'And is it true that the Claytons have been asked for a ran-som?'

'Haven't a clue. It's not our case, after all. All we know at the station is what we get on the grapevine.'

'It is a sad business.'

'Yes indeed.'

They went out of the room, and as they were descending, Myra asked, 'That chauffeur then, he could have driven the car away himself?'

'There is that possibility.'

In the hall the detective said, 'Well, I've seen everything, haven't I?'

'There is the garage.'

'Oh yes. Might as well do that too. Is your car in or out?'

'We have not got a car. I am afraid we cannot afford one.'

They went outside and Myra unlocked the garage. The detective looked at the ceiling, at the nail-hanging tools on the walls and at the floor. The cement floor was crisscrossed with tyre marks.

Myra said, 'My husband's old motor-bike.'

Beedle nodded, and asked, 'It's William Savage, isn't it?'

'That is right. William Henry Savage.'

He nodded again and turned away, and Myra slammed the door to. The detective said, 'Well, I think that's it. I hope I haven't put you to too much trouble.'

'None at all.'

'Well, thank you for being so co-operative, Mrs.Savage.'

'My pleasure. And please give my regards to your wife.'

'Thank you, I will. Good morning.' He gave her a final smile and walked through the gateless gateway.

Myra said, 'Good morning,' and went back into the house. Standing in the lounge she watched the car shunt twice back and forth across the road to turn. When it disappeared from view she let out a long sigh of relief, glad that the visit was over, and glad that it had been a lot easier than expected. She felt the faintly suspicious attitude the policeman had shown at times was just the normal one all policemen had, on duty or off, and that he was completely satisfied. As she went through to the back to get the bedsheet she was humming softly.

Bill had driven almost to Romford before turning back and heading in toward the city. He dawdled along on quiet roads and had another cup of tea, and in East Ham stopped and sat on his bike to wait. The seconds ticked by so slowly that it seemed eleven o'clock would never come; but it finally did. He moved on again and found a deserted side street.

After making sure he was not observed he opened the side-car, poured a drop of chloroform on to his handkerchief and gave the sleeping child a few whiffs. He shook her shoulder gently; she didn't stir. He snapped the cover down and drove on.

Cutting over to the Mile End Road he began to look for somewhere to leave the bike. He wanted a parking place that was in a busy and noisy spot; busy to prevent a thief from sneaking around and looking in the side-car, and noisy to drown any sounds the girl might make should she moan in her sleep, or waken and cry; it also had to be a legal parking spot, where there would be no fear of the police nosing about. At length he found the perfect place. It was in full view of a row of shops, and close to a light-controlled intersection. The traffic roared by constantly.

He put his goggles and gloves inside his helmet, which he strapped tight up against the handlebar, and left the bike without looking back and walked to a cab rank. Glancing at his watch he was startled to see that whereas the time had crept before, it galloped now; it was already eleven-thirty. He got in a cab and told the driver to take him, quickly, to Oxford Circus.

The taxi moved off, and Bill soon saw there was no hope of going quickly; the traffic had become dense, and was moving in spurts and crawls. He looked at his watch every time the cab changed speed, and felt sure he'd be late, and cursed himself for waiting so long in East Ham. When it was a quarter to twelve he began to get seriously worried and asked the driver if there wasn't a short cut. The driver said no, there wasn't.

It was seven minutes to twelve and the taxi was moving slowly up Charing Cross Road. Bill banged on the glass, said, 'Here, this'll do,' and was out almost before the cab had stopped. He thrust money at the driver, turned away quickly and walked to the nearest side street, and entered Soho.

He came to a fruiterer's shop, but it was crowded, and he strode past it briskly and began looking for another. He saw instead a barrow offering an assortment of fruits, and hurried to it and bought six oranges, three of which he put into each coat pocket, squeezing them in against the folded cap in one and the plastic pack in the other.

It was four minutes to twelve. He walked to Shaftesbury Avenue, crossed it, went into Gerrard Street, turned a corner and stopped. Bringing the blue cap out he clamped it on his head and pulled the peak right down on to his eyebrows, and looked at his reflection in a shop window. The cap changed his appearance even more than the grease-flattening of the hair had done. With still less counter-balance now that the forehead was gone, the lower face seemed to be all nose. He was even a little startled himself.

Hurrying on he came into Coventry Street and turned left. He began to slow, and came to a stop when Leicester Square started to open up before him. Fifty feet away was the west corner of the square. Standing around the row of telephone kiosks were several men, one of whom, dressed in a black overcoat and black bowler, was holding a blue bag that had a small white package tied to its handles. Bill didn't know what the white package meant, but he recognized the man, from Myra's description of him, as Clayton.

The other men waiting on the corner didn't worry him; he felt that the police, were they involved, would not make themselves so obvious.

It was twelve o'clock. The man with the blue bag looked at his wrist-watch and took a step closer to the end kiosk, but made no move to go inside it. Bill frowned, till he saw the reason: the booth was occupied.

The streets began to fill with people, moving swiftly in all directions. The offices were emptying. The pavement in front of Clayton became crowded, which, joined with the fact that the traffic was dense, made it difficult for Bill to keep him in sight. He moved a few steps closer and stood on the kerb, and saw Clayton glance at his watch and rap on the glass of the kiosk.

Bill suddenly felt he was being watched, and swung his head quickly to face the opposite side of the street. There was a man there, wearing a green trilby, standing in a shop doorway and gazing in at the window display. Bill was sure the man had been looking at him a second before, and had turned away just in time. But perhaps, he thought hopefully, it was only imagination.

He looked back toward the square. Clayton was gone. Bill started nervously, and craned his neck to see. But his view became blocked. When a break came in the traffic he caught a quick glimpse of the blue and white of the bag; it was inside the phone booth.

Turning abruptly he hurried to the first corner, and stopped just around it. After waiting half a minute he looked back on to Coventry Street. The man with the green hat was still by the doorway, and facing in the opposite direction. Bill turned away, satisfied.

There was a vacant telephone kiosk outside the post office in Gerrard Street. He entered it. His heart was thudding, and he took a deep breath and told himself to calm down. Forcing his movements to be leisurely, he brought out coins and a slip of paper. On the paper was the number of the phone in Leicester Square; he'd taken it down a week before.

He lifted the receiver, fed the coin slot and dialled. His heart thudded again when the ring was answered with, 'Yes?'

Bill said, 'This is Longfellow.'

A sigh, and, dully, 'Yes.'

'Listen carefully. As soon as I've rung off you will walk along Coventry Street to Piccadilly Circus. Do not speak to anyone or signal. You will be watched. You are being watched now. You have been watched all morning. I can see you at this moment, in your black bowler hat and black coat. If you speak to anyone, or . . .'

'*Please*,' the voice cut in urgently. 'I'm not going to speak to anyone. The police aren't in on this. I swear it. Just tell me where to take the money. All I . . .'

'All right, shut up,' Bill said, glad to be callous, glad to stop the pleading voice. 'Go to Piccadilly Circus and go down to the Underground. Buy a ticket to Uxbridge. Go down the escalators. At the bottom is a hall surrounded by passages. Wait there. A man will come up to you and say "Longfellow". Give him the bag immediately. Don't speak to him, just hand over the bag. Got all that?'

'Yes, I've got it.'

'Repeat it.'

'Wait in the hall at the bottom of the escalators and give the bag to the man who says "Longfellow".'

'Right. You know what'll happen to your kid if there's any interference, so for her sake there'd better not be any cops around.'

'The police don't even know about this. Believe me.'

'Right, get going. Don't waste time.' He dropped the receiver quickly, fearful of another spurt of pleading, and gave it a rough wipe with his handkerchief.

Leaving the kiosk he walked briskly west along Gerrard Street. As he tore up the slip of paper bearing the phone number, letting the tiny pieces float away behind him, he wondered if it could be true what Clayton had said, that the police had not been informed of the transaction. He hoped it was. He was beginning to feel that his scheme for getting the money was not as foolproof as he'd thought when working it out on paper in the security of his living-room. Several things had occurred to him that hadn't occurred to him before.

He came to the end of the street and turned right. Glancing up at the sky, he slowed and moved to the inside of the pavement, where he stopped and gave his full attention to the grey but dry-looking heavens. He held out a hand, palm up. Nodding, as though having reached a decision, he eased the plastic pack carefully past the oranges and out of his pocket, and unfolded it and shook it out. It was a raincoat, blue and dimly transparent, patterned in squares by the creases of the folds.

As he put the coat on he glanced around, and saw that no one was taking the slightest notice of him. This, besides pleasing him, gave him a small feeling of triumph, since he had argued it would be so, and that changing in the phone booth, as Myra had suggested, would have been peculiar in dry weather, and noticed by passers-by.

He moved on, snapping together the press-studs up the front of the coat. In a mirror inside a furniture shop window he got a quick flash of an ugly stark-white face, and was shocked and faintly hurt when he realized it was his own.

Turning into Shaftesbury Avenue he walked swiftly, with long knee-sagging strides, to Piccadilly Circus and added himself to the throng going down the subway steps. The station was crowded with the noon rush, as he knew it would be, and he joined the shortest queue—three people—of the many in front of the ticket machines. While waiting he had a careful look around, but saw no sign of Clayton.

He bought a threepenny ticket and walked slowly with the crowd toward the escalators. Two were on the descent, and he got on the one nearest the middle. When he curved over, down from the level, he could see the hall far below. It was thickly bordered with bustling people, moving in and out of the passages that led into it, leaving a clear space in the centre.

In the space was Clayton, one hand pocketed, the other holding the bag, standing quite still and staring down at the ground near the foot of the stairs. His face had an unhealthy pallor. He looked lost.

Bill felt pity welling up in him, and quickly hardened his mind against his heart. He looked away, to the right-hand side of the hall below. The wall had two tunnel-like mouths, and the closer of the two was swallowing up a thick wedge of people fed to it from the stairs and other passages; the farther one was completely free, and was marked above NO ENTRY.

He was nearing the bottom, and could see clearly the dark shadows under Clayton's eyes and the blank expression on his face, when out of the side of his vision he thought he saw a green hat among the many heads, and he turned and stared hard. But suddenly the escalator swooped out on to the straight, and he couldn't see over the taller people around him. He couldn't even see Clayton.

He moved to the first passage, and entered it at little more than a shuffle. The pace quickened to a walk once inside, and he pushed forward, one hand touching the back of the man in front. He was hoping he might just be in time for the next train.

The passage ended and the people fanned out on to the platform and began to spread themselves along beside the drop to the rails. Bill hurried the few yards to the empty entrance of the second passage, and stopped, and stood listening. He had spent two hours here several days before, and had learned to judge from the sound of approaching trains just how long it would be before they flashed out of the black mouth of the tunnel.

He looked down the passage, an elongated arch of shining white tiles and gradually shrinking posters. Fifty feet in it curved gently to the left, and around the curve was, he knew, the hall, and Clayton. He fixed his eyes on the first poster, a woman's face with the teeth blackly removed by someone's pencil, and fought against the faint panic that was rising in him. This was the time he'd feared right from the conception of the Plan; the actual contact.

He stared hard at the poster, and found himself wondering what the artist must think when he saw his creation disfigured this way.

His every muscle tightened. He'd heard a distant rumbling. Of its own accord his head tilted toward the sound, reaching for it. The rumbling grew, and was joined by a whining, and then by a clanging. The noise swelled to a pitch he recognized, and he broke abruptly from his standing position and strode quickly into the passage.

At once the noise diminished; but after he'd taken six steps it burst into double strength behind him, and he knew that the train had come out of the tunnel. He lengthened his stride.

He turned the bend and came out into the hall. Clayton was still in the same spot, facing the other way, facing the stairs. Bill went straight to his side, jerked to a stop, held out his hand and said . . . nothing; he couldn't speak.

Clayton started and turned. His eyes, staring and haunted, were so shot with blood they were pink. His mouth worked loosely as he gasped, 'Longfellow?'

Bill could only nod.

Clayton's body shrank back slightly and his arm came forward with the bag.

Bill took it, almost crying out as his hand touched the other man's, and made a swift, awkward swing round and strode toward the passage he'd just left. He breathed in, suddenly and deeply, and realized he'd been holding his breath.

Inside the passage he broke into a run, a mad run, pulling up the bag and clutching it to his chest. The tiles threw back an amplified and multiplied clattering of his footsteps; it sounded like ten men running.

He reached the end of the passage just as the train's disgorged horde bore down on it, and he only barely squeezed through on to the platform before the tide became too strong for him to fight against.

Glancing behind he thought he saw, but wasn't sure, a green trilby bobbing frantically atop the mob.

He moved quickly to the train, to the end door of a compartment, and got aboard, pushing in close among the crowd inside. Holding the bag to his chest with one hand, he used the other hand to rip apart the press-studs of the plastic coat.

The doors hissed to, there was a jerk, and the train moved away. Bill turned, casually removing his cap, to face the corner made by the door and the wall. Working so his movements, if possible, would not be noticed from behind, he pulled out the folded carrier bag, opened it, pushed the blue bag inside—awkwardly, the white package catching on the string handles—and dropped his cap in on top. He lowered the bundle to the floor and trapped it between his legs.

He looked over his shoulder. The crowd had thinned, as some had moved into the compartment proper and found seats. There were two men a yard away, their backs turned, and at an arm's length another man was reading a newspaper.

Bill began to take off the plastic macintosh, wincing at the crackling and whistling noise it made. He'd got his left arm free and was twisting to free the right one when he saw that the man with the newspaper was watching. But as soon as the man realized his observing was known, he raised his eyebrows and turned back to his paper.

Bill pulled the macintosh off, and hiding it before him crumpled it roughly into a ball. As he lifted the carrier bag and stuffed the coat into it the train suddenly burst into a station and began slowing.

Quickly now, careless of whether he was seen or not, he brought the oranges from his pockets and lay them in the bag on top of the macintosh. They just nicely filled the space and were set about an inch down. He was surprised at the perfection.

The train stopped, the doors rolled back, and he stepped out on to the platform of Leicester Square station. Running a hand through his hair to make sure it wasn't flattened, he moved with the crowd to the exit passage. His eyes flicked around everywhere, but he saw no signs of anything that looked like a policeman; but he knew that that didn't necessarily mean there weren't any.

He felt like chasing up the escalator, to keep in tune with the rapid beat of his heart, but he forced himself to stand at the side and be carried up slowly. However, when half-way to the top he couldn't contain himself any longer, and began to walk.

He passed through the barrier, went to a corner of the crowded station and trotted casually up a flight of steps. He came out at street level, at a corner of Charing Cross Road, and lowering the carrier bag to his side started to stroll at a leisurely pace, heading away from the corner, heading north.

After a dozen steps he stopped and turned fully round.

Everything seemed quite normal. He was turning again when a vacant taxi sped by, and he hailed it, and walked quickly to it as it skidded to a halt a little way ahead. He got in, telling the driver, 'Mile End, please,' and knelt on the seat and watched through the rear window. Then he realized that the cabbie might find his position singular, and remember him because of it, and he turned and sat correctly, contenting himself with an occasional glance back.

His body felt sticky, and he worked his fingers under the six layers of clothing and touched his skin. It was slippery with sweat, and he didn't even feel warm.

He decided that it was all over, finished, completed, the pick-up of the money successfully accomplished, and that he could relax. But he still sat stiff, unyielding to the seat, holding the bag on his close-clamped knees.

His mind turned to Clayton's face, the haunted look and the anguished eyes. He hastily thought of something else. He thought of the whole pick-up, from the phone call to the emergence in Leicester Square; of the man in the green hat, who might have been a policeman and might have been trying to follow, forcing his way through the crowd in the exit passage; of the man with the newspaper who'd seen him take off his coat. He re-lived the event, every detail of it vivid in his mind, and finished back at Clayton's face. He knew he'd never forget that face.

He was startled when the cabbie asked, 'Where 'bouts on Mile End?' and he looked out of the window and saw that they were approaching the cross-roads where he'd left the bike. He said, 'Through the lights and it's the first turn left.'

The cab put on a burst of speed to catch the green signal, and they were across the junction. Bill looked at his machine standing on the other side of the road; everything seemed in order.

When the taxi swung into a side street Bill said, 'This'll do.' He got out, kept his head tilted down while he paid the driver, and walked back on to the main road, cradling the carrier bag in one arm.

He reached the bike and stood close beside it, his senses focused on the side-car. There was no sound, no movement. With his free hand he cautiously unsnapped a corner of the waterproof, glanced around, and peered in. He could see, among the blanket folds, part of the nose and the open mouth of Adriana. He could also see and smell that she'd been sick. As he unfastened more of the cover he sighed sympathetically.

He lay the bag on its side behind the child, unmindful of the running of the oranges, and replaced the waterproof. The engine started on the second kick. He donned helmet, goggles and gloves and swung on to the saddle, and steered away from the kerb. As he stopped at the junction's red light he looked at his watch; it was ten minutes to one.

At one-thirty, having avoided the centre of the city, he was half-way home, driving at exactly the legal speed limit along a secondary road that wound through suburban residential areas. He came to a busy shopping district, and slowed slightly.

The bike engine coughed, chugged, stopped, started again, coughed again, and stopped altogether. The machine dribbled to a halt a yard out from the kerb. Bill looked at the fuel gauge; it showed empty. He clicked his tongue with annoy-ance and got to the ground, thinking that the slow driving he'd done all morning was responsible for the heavy con-sumption of petrol.

He grasped the handlebars, leaned over them and began to push, steering closer to the side of the road. The machine barely moved. He put his head down and pitted all his weight against the handlebars. The wheels started to turn slowly.

Suddenly they were turning quickly. He looked up and glanced behind. A policeman was helping to push, one hand on the pillion and one on the side-car.

Bill twisted to face the front, his mouth drying, and had to jerk the bars frantically to keep the bike from running up the kerb. He braked to a stop, and straightened slowly, composing his face. He turned, forcing his lips to draw back from his teeth.

The policeman was brushing his hands together. He was young and gaunt-faced, and thin, his neck needing two inches more to fill his collar. He said, 'Petrol?'

Bill managed to give an affirmative grunt.

'I thought so. Knew by the sound. I'm a B.S.A. man myself. Mine's only two year old though.'

Bill was standing almost at attention, his feet touching and his arms straight at his sides. His artificial smile was like the grimace one produces unconsciously while watching someone suffer.

The policeman said, 'This one's an old 'un, isn't she?'

Bill moistened his mouth before saying, before being able to say, 'Yes, fourteen years.'

'Got guts though, the old 'uns.' He put his hands behind

and one foot forward, and shrugged down his shoulders comfortably. 'Nice big side-car too.'

'Petrol . . . where can . . .?'

'Just there. Fifty yards away. Nice and handy.'

Bill forced himself to move. He stepped up the kerb.

The constable said, 'Mate of mine's got a Norton, and you know what he reckons?'

Before Bill's confused brain could tell him how to answer, there was a noise from the side-car; a drawn out scraping noise. It was followed by a light thud. He shuddered violently.

'Got something in there?' the constable asked, his face showing mild curiosity.

Bill, dominated by guilt, translated the mild curiosity as hard cold suspicion. But he had an answer ready; one prepared for just such an emergency: a vicious dog. He said, instead, he didn't know why, 'Two cats.'

'Oh. Sick, are they?'

Bill turned half to the side. 'Yes.' His legs were trembling, the thighs painful. 'Hurry.' He began to walk away.

'Just a minute.'

Bill stopped, suddenly and with a gasp. He started to turn slowly, his feet shuffling round.

The policeman said, 'You're going the wrong way. It's back here.'

Bill's legs began to tremble more than ever. He stumbled forward and moved past the constable, hearing as he did another thud from the side-car.

'Just there,' the policeman said. 'Set back behind the end shop.'

Bill walked on, picking up speed. It took real will power to prevent him from running. All he wanted to do was get away, far away, from the bike and the policeman. At that moment he didn't care about the child or the money or his wife; he just wanted to get away; he couldn't stand any more tension.

He reached the end shop and turned the corner, and was on the forecourt of a service station. He stopped, and tried to bring coherence to his jumbled thoughts, forcing himself to be sensible and calculating. He lifted his shaking hands to his face, and touching the goggles made him realize that at least he was well covered.

But, he thought, the policeman would certainly remember the incident of the noisy side-car, and perhaps because of it the number of the bike, and put two and two together if it came out that such a vehicle could have been involved in the affair; he might be putting two and two together at this very moment. And at any moment Adriana might shout.

Again Bill wanted to run, and he had to fight hard against the temptation. Instead he moved quickly to the petrol pumps, to the side of the girl attendant, who, he suddenly noted, was watching him curiously. He mumbled hurriedly, galloping his words together, that he wanted some petrol in a can. He was only vaguely aware of what the girl said, and that she had fetched a can and was starting to fill it; he'd been stupefied by another chilling thought: what if the constable lifted the waterproof to peep at the cats?

The girl handed him a one-gallon can, and he handed her a ten-shilling note—with surprise; he hadn't known he'd taken it out of his pocket. He turned and walked back to the corner, where he stopped and eased his upper body carefully forward to see how things stood.

The policeman was near the bike but with his back to it, talking to a white-aproned shopkeeper. Bill stepped out on to the pavement.

He didn't even glance at the constable as he approached, and moved into the road to walk diagonally to the far side of his machine so as to put more space between them. Removing the tops from the fuel tank and can, he began pouring out the petrol, the convulsive spewing of the can's mouth and his own nervousness spilling more fluid over the tank than in it.

Before the can was fully empty he pulled it away, replaced the tank top, and squatted down to put some petrol in the carburettor bowl. He was loosening the screw under the bowl, awkwardly with his gloved fingers, when there was another sound from the side-car; a long, low moan.

He didn't dare look at the policeman. He clenched his teeth and twisted the screw viciously. The bowl sagged, and he pulled it from its seat and mechanically wiped the sediment from it with his thumb before splashing it full of petrol. He replaced it, tightened it, picked up the can and cap and moved quickly away, not fully straightening his body till he'd covered several yards. The cap jumped from his hand as he tried to twist it on, and he chased it madly to the gutter and caught it.

The girl attendant was standing at the corner, watching. He reached her, thrust her the can, took the change from her outstretched hand, swung around quickly, put the money in his pocket, walked in long strides back to the bike, switched on the ignition, pulled down the kick pedal and kicked. The engine sputtered, coughed and died.

The policeman had turned from the shopkeeper and was standing close to the side-car. He said, 'Cats make queer noises, don't they? Just like babies.'

Bill managed a smiling nod, and kicked again. The engine caught and roared. He got in the saddle, nodded again as the policeman touched his helmet, and moved off with a mighty jerk.

He'd travelled barely fifty yards when the waterproof was banged up in the centre, and Adriana's voice sounded clearly above the engine, shouting in a fear-tinged voice, 'Where am I?' He revved loudly and put on speed, and in a minute was out of the shopping district and out of sight of the policeman. Adriana went on shouting.

The road was quiet, a field on one hand and a dusty-looking works on the other. Bill came to a fast stop, leaned to the side and vomited. His stomach muscles tore harshly at one another and his eyes burned hotly, but he was soon finished, and, looking up at the sky and gulping, felt much better, the tension gone, but replaced by a pressing weariness.

The waterproof was knocked up again. Bill hit the place hard, by letting gravity pull down his uplifted, tired arm, and summoned all his energy to shout, 'Be quiet!' Silence and stillness from the side-car. He drove on, picking up speed rapidly, and thought about nothing except how much better he felt.

Myra was getting nervous. The estimated time of Bill's return was two o'clock. Now it was ten past. With her imagination suggesting many things, from a fatal accident to an arrest, she had spent the past quarter-hour moving back and forth between the front and rear windows, staying no more than a minute at each, glad to have the comfort of movement and the work of opening and closing the door from lounge to kitchen.

The time had passed quickly since the police visit. She had put the plywood back in both windows, given the house a rough clean, had a snack, and chatted for a while with a woman who had called to make an appointment for a private séance on Friday next. Myra had smiled, watching the woman leave, thinking that soon there would be queues for appointments, and perhaps a secretary to handle them.

She was standing at the sink, looking over the fields to the back of the housing estate, hoping to catch a glimpse of the motor-bike as her husband came to look for the bedsheet signal, when she heard the growl of an engine, and recognized it. Rushing back to the front of the house, smiling with relief, she went outside just as Bill reached the gate. She swung open the garage and followed the bike inside, blinking at the trebled noise from the exhaust.

Bill switched off the engine, pulled his hands from the bars, and sagged, his chin sinking to his chest. The smile went from Myra's face as she came round to front him. She asked, 'What is the matter? Anything wrong?'

He began to shake his head, but quickly lifted it, jerking his body upright, and raised a forefinger to his mouth. He climbed from the saddle and backed out, beckoning. Myra followed worriedly.

'She's awake,' he whispered, pulling off his gloves.

'How do you know?'

'She's been shouting.'

'How long has she been awake?'

'A good half-hour.'

'Did anyone hear?'

'No.' He removed the goggles an began to unstrap the helmet. 'And she's been sick.'

Myra could see that he'd had a hard time; his face seemed to have shrunk a little. She asked, 'Nothing went wrong, did it?'

'No. Everything worked perfectly.'

She glanced back inside the garage, and said, 'Do you think she knows she is in a motor-bike?'

He blinked. 'My God! I never thought of that.'

She nodded. 'We shall soon know. You wait here. I will go and change.' She went into the house, up the stairs, and quickly donned the white dress and tied the handkerchief over her hair. Downstairs again she went through to the rear, leaving the doors open, and round to the front. She said, panting slightly, 'You keep out of sight.'

Bill moved behind the open half of the garage door, and glanced up the road. Apart from a small boy on a tricycle at the far end, the street was deserted.

With her upper body bent horizontally above the side-car and as close to it as possible, Myra unsnapped the cover and pulled it back. Adriana lay partly covered by the twisted blanket, and was staring up with angry and frightened eyes. She said, 'Where am I?' Myra ignored the question, and swiftly re-wrapped the child, covering her head, and lifted her out.

Bill waited till his wife's footsteps died away at the rear of the house before he went in the garage. He picked up the carrier bag and slowly put the escaped oranges into its top, sighing down wearily at the mess the child had made. In the house he walked straight through to the kitchen, where he placed the bag on the bottom shelf of a tall cupboard, standing it upright against a saucepan.

After throwing aside the soiled blanket Myra settled Adriana in the bed, tucking her in comfortably. She sat down and asked, 'Feel better?'

The child nodded, the fear and anger gone from her eyes. She was subdued, and seemed glad to be back in familiar surroundings. She said, 'I'm hungry.'

'Do you know where you have been?'

Adriana frowned. 'Well . . .'

'I will tell you. You have been in a special cabinet, for treatment. Did you ever see a picture of an iron lung? Well, the cabinet is something like that, but it makes a lot of noise and shakes about. It is the vibration that gives the treatment.'

Adriana didn't look too interested. She said, 'It made me sick.'

'It is supposed to.'

'I thought it was an aeroplane.'

Myra laughed and stood up. 'Soon I will bring you something to eat. And in the morning, if you have been a good little girl, you can go home.' She left the room, taking the soiled blanket with her and dropping it in the bath with the other dirty linen.

In the kitchen she set the kettle on the stove, brought out

a loaf, and looked into the lounge to ask her husband what he wanted to eat. Bill was sitting in his chair, leaning back with eyes closed. His coat, helmet, goggles and gloves had been thrown carelessly on the couch, and Myra raised her eyebrows at them and knew now for certain that he'd had a nerve-wracking morning. She asked, 'Did you clean out the side-car?'

He opened his eyes and began to pull himself forward. 'No. I forgot.'

'All right. Sit still. I will attend to it.' She took a floor-cloth out to the garage and cleaned the whole of the side-car's interior, cleaning the mess and removing any fingerprints the child might have left. She lifted out the chloroform bottle, tutting at her husband's laxity in forgetting it, and took it with her into the house.

In the lounge she asked, 'What do you want to eat?'

Bill said, 'Nothing, thanks. Not hungry.'

She shrugged, and joined him at the hearth. 'What happened? You got the money?'

He sat up. 'Yes. I put it in the kitchen cupboard.'

'Tell me everything,' she said, folding her arms and sitting down. 'Did he speak to you?'

Bill told her the events of the morning, starting and ending with the parking place in the Mile End Road. He told her every detail, not forgetting the man with the green hat. He didn't mention the incident with the policeman, knowing she would be angry with him for not remembering to fill up the fuel tank; he couldn't stand her anger; it took the form of complete silence, cold and forbidding, and sometimes lasted for days.

She said, 'Well, that seems fine. Nothing went wrong as far as I can judge. And you saw the signal all right?'

'Signal?'

'That the bedsheet had gone from the back.'

'Oh yes. Yes, I saw.' He'd forgotten the sheet till now. He felt his face redden, and said quickly, 'So the police came then? What did they have to say?'

Myra tilted her head as she heard the thin squeak of the kettle's whistle. She rose. 'I will make the girl a bite to eat and then tell you about the police—it was nothing—and what the detective said about the Clayton's chauffeur. It will probably be in the evening paper.'

At seven o'clock Myra came downstairs. The people would be arriving soon for the regular Wednesday night séance, and she had just finished preparing for them. She had washed, combed her hair and rubbed a tinge of black from an ordinary lead pencil into her scar to deepen it. The preparation in the séance room consisted of switching on the light, covering the window and placing a candle in a china holder in the centre of the table. She had gone in quietly to the girl's room, and found her asleep, and had left the chloroform and a cloth under the bed for her husband to use, should it be necessary, should there be any noise to waken the child—which was unlikely; people were generally church-quiet at séances.

The light was on in the hall, and as she reached the foot of the stairs she saw that the newspaper was sticking through the letter slot. She pulled it out and opened it. The large headline said RANSOM PAID FOR CLAYTON GIRL. There was a picture of Adriana, a blurred one of her father, frowning heavily, and a studio portrait of her mother, taken in débutante days; at the bottom of the column was a small picture of a middle-aged man. Myra quickly read the story, nodded, and went into the living-room.

Her husband was asleep in his chair. He'd been asleep for two hours; which, thought Myra, was long enough. She coughed loudly, switched on the light and drew and pinned the curtains.

Bill came awake, sucking in a deep breath and stretching open his eyes, and smiled when he saw that he was safely at home; he'd been having a frightening dream of being chased by green-faced men down labyrinthine ways. He felt rested now and not so depressed, and leaned forward eagerly as his wife sat in her chair, his eyes on the paper in her hands.

She said, 'Listen,' and began to read aloud. *'At twelve o'clock noon today Mr. Charles Clayton of . . .* etcetera . . . *paid the sum of twenty-five thousand pounds to an unknown person for the return of his daughter, Adriana, who was kidnapped on Monday while on her way home from school. Mr. and Mrs. Clayton are now awaiting the return of their only child. The police were not informed of the time and place of the meeting with the man who collected the ransom, since it was stated in a letter from the kidnappers that harm might befall the girl if any attempts were made to apprehend the collector. At two o'clock today Mr. Clayton issued a statement at his home in Barnet. He said the money, in a small handbag bearing the initials B.O.A.C., was handed to a man in Piccadilly Underground station. The man made off down a no-entry passage leading from a platform just as a train came in, making it almost impossible for anyone to give chase through the outward rush of out-going passengers. Mr. Clayton was unable to give a description of the man. The chauffeur to the Claytons, Henry Webster, who was with . . . etcetera . . . was taken to Barnet police station today to help with the investigation.'* She lowered the paper and looked at her husband. 'Help with the investigation?'

Bill said, 'That means he's unofficially arrested.'

'That is what I thought.' She lifted the paper again and ran her eyes down the column, saying, 'The rest of it is about the Claytons and the school.'

'Does it say anything about the car they're looking for?'

'Ummm, oh yes, here. But it is just the same as in this morning's paper. A small car of about eight horse-power. Where did they get that idea from, and what happened to the green van they wanted?'

Bill told her his assumption about the tracks left by his motor-cycle in the field. She looked pleased; so pleased that he was tempted for a moment to tell her of his escapade with the constable; but only for a moment. He said, 'As a matter of fact, I had an idea right from the first that they'd think that.'

'Let us hope they go on thinking it.' She handed him the newspaper.

His eye was caught by the small photo at the foot of the column. He looked at it for a moment, and asked, 'I wonder what they'll do with the chauffeur?'

She shrugged. 'Let him go, sooner or later. They could not do anything to an innocent man. It is only a temporary thing.'

'I hope so. Wouldn't it be awful if they somehow proved he was mixed up in it.'

She shrugged again and looked at the clock. 'It is nearly time.'

He rose to his feet and stretched. 'I'll wash my hands and face.'

'And I will put your things away.' She followed him from the hearth, and collected his clothes off the couch and carried them into the kitchen. After fixing the curtains and putting on the light she sat at the table and folded her hands in her lap. She would wait now till everyone was in the séance room, before making her entrance.

Bill had a quick wash, combed his hair and straightened his tie, and brushed the dandruff off his collar. Halfway through the bathroom door he stopped, frowned, and looked back. Hurrying down the stairs he poked his head inside the kitchen, just as the knocker on the front door was banged.

He said to his wife, 'What if someone wants to go to the toilet?'

'Well?'

'They'll see the plywood.'

'Oh yes.' She frowned thoughtfully, and said, 'It is rare that that happens, but it might. I shall say that everything in the bathroom has been painted and is still wet.'

He nodded and turned away. Walking quickly to the front door he swung it wide and said, 'Good evening. Please come in.'

'Evenin', Mr. Savage,' said a black-clad woman of about seventy. She fiddled with a flashlight and switched it off. 'Nippy.'

'Yes, Mrs. George, it is a bit.' He reached out and took her arm to help her over the step. 'But spring's around the corner.'

She walked slowly past him and went to the foot of the stairs, saying happily, 'There 'asn't been no springs for me since my Alfie crossed the Rubicon.'

Bill said, 'Ah.' He took her arm again and they began to climb, side by side and closely clamped, his shoulder blade sliding along the wall. He ushered her into the séance room, gritting his teeth at the noise their feet made on the bare boards, sat her down and left her regaining her breath.

In the next fifteen minutes four more women, all middle-aged to old, came to the door, were greeted by name and taken upstairs. When he came down after the last arrival, Bill looked at his wrist-watch, checked it by the living-room clock, and turned toward the kitchen.

A knock sounded on the front door. Bill swung about smartly and opened it.

A tall well-groomed and expensively dressed woman stood blinking at the light. She was, Bill thought, about thirty. She was pretty, and her long hair was almost white. She said, 'Am I too late for the séance?'

'No. In perfect time, actually. Won't you come in, Mrs . . .?'

'Clayton.'

The name hit Bill like a punch in the chest; his head and shoulders jerked back. He stared at the woman searchingly as she came past him into the hall, and flicked his eyes away as she turned. Closing the door carefully, using both hands, as though it were not an easy task, he composed his features into something as close to blandness as he could get, telling himself that there was nothing to fear, that the woman had only come in answer to Myra's invitation and couldn't possibly have any suspicions.

He turned around, mumbled, 'Will you come this way, please,' and led the way upstairs. In the séance room he introduced her quickly to the other women, only one of whom, he noted, showed any interest in the name of the newcomer. He made a gesture to show that it was time to start, and the women rose from their chairs and carried them quietly to the table, he following with a chair for Myra. There was the usual polite and apparently unintentional manœuvring to get a place directly next to the medium's, and then they were seated. Bill put a match to the candle, switched off the ceiling light and went out. He hurried down to the kitchen and threw open the door.

He said, 'Guess who's here?'

Myra, rising from the table, frowned thoughtfully, and said, 'Mr. Clayton.'

'No,' he said, disappointed that she'd come so close, and without surprise. 'Mrs. Clayton.'

'Oh.' Myra was disappointed too. She had been thrilled for a second with the prospect of sitting in séance with Charles Clayton, but his young wife had no para-normal gifts whatever.

Bill said, 'You don't suppose she knows anything, do you?'

'Of course not. I have been hoping one of them would come. It strengthens my connexion with the affair.' She walked past him. 'But you had better keep a close watch on the child.'

They went upstairs and separated, she to the front room and he to the back. Bill closed the door gently behind him and tiptoed across to the bed. The dim light showed him Adriana's upturned face, vacant and openmouthed in sleep; a sleep that seemed deep enough, he thought, not to need the aid of chloroform. He smiled as he carefully, and unnecessarily, tucked the blankets around her ears. He felt a kinship existed between them, as though they had been through the events of the day side-by-side, sharing the danger. Tenderly he stroked the black hair, and thought she was a sweet little girl really.

He heard faintly the scrape of a chair, and left the bed abruptly and went to the wall. With one hand he moved the picture and with the other followed it, ready to cover the peep-hole and keep the light from penetrating the other room. When the picture was firmly in place upside down he put his eye to the hole.

Myra stood at the head of the table, and thought it would be a very ordinary séance indeed. None of the women had the slightest hint of psychic power. It would be just a routine job of trying with the subconscious mind, failing, and improvising with the conscious mind, making banal and vague but encouraging statements.

There were three women on either side, the farthest on her left Mrs. Clayton. Before sitting down Myra greeted each of them by name, adding to the woman from Barnet, 'Nice to see you here.'

The candle—more evidence of Myra's mediumistic unconventionality—threw seven large, gently waving shadows on the walls; shadows whose shoulders lifted in response to Myra's command, 'Let us make a circle.' Hands were clasped all round on the table, and one or two pairs of eyes were closed, and the séance was on.

Myra, her fingers lying loosely in hands at either side, fixed her gaze straight ahead, a few inches above the flame of the candle, and began to concentrate. Even though she knew there would be nothing for her subliminal to work on, she gave it, as she always did, a chance to try; she felt it her duty to do so. First she cleared her mind of everything, especially the fact that she was being closely and awesomely watched, and forgot space, time and herself.

The friendly glow of the candle worked like a hypnotist's bauble on her senses. Her mind became a complete blank, not even holding the thought of what she was trying to do. She began to feel drowsy. Her eyelids dropped, her mouth sagged, and she was floating into a trance. . . .

She walked along the corridor, smiling; smiling both at her happiness at being back in a well-loved place, and at the faded yellow that coloured the walls in such an endearing way that it made her heart ache with sweet melancholy. The colour soothed, caressed, drew her on, on to where the corridor ended in a large door, at the sight of which her smile widened. She came closer, and saw every detail of the door's surface: the unpainted grey wood, the knots and whorls, the crack down the centre of each panel, the white knob with the black ring where the porcelain was worn away. When a dozen feet from it she stopped, was stopped, was held back firmly by something behind her. The smile went. She tried with all her mind, but there was no going forward, and she sighed and gazed longingly at the door. Then she started to glide backwards, slowly, evenly . . . back . . . back. . . .

Gradually Myra came aware that the attempt was over. She sat perfectly still and kept her eyes closed. It was as she had expected; there was not enough mental co-operation even to take her to the door, let alone beyond it. If she could have reached it, touched it, she would have been able to receive telepathic messages. Beyond it anything was possible. She had been beyond it three times, but only for fleeting seconds, but those seconds were the happiest of her life. She breathed a heavy sigh, for herself and for the benefit of the watchers, and turned her mind to the task in hand.

She said, 'I have a message for someone on my left. Someone who has a business problem.'

'Yes.' said a trembling voice. 'That's me.'

Myra knew the voice belonged to a Mrs. Wintry, who owned more than a hundred old houses, most of them condemned, and who spent her time fighting tenants and the council. She said, 'You are worried about some property.'

'Yes.'

'It is old property, but sound and good for many years.'

'Oh yes.'

'There are persons involved who would hurt you if they could.'

'Yes, there are.'

'I get a strong feeling of uneasiness coming from these people. They are waiting for a decision, a decision you must make.'

'By Friday noon.'

'The message I have for you is very explicit. You must . . .'

'Who is it from?'

'You must take into account the prevailing conditions in property, follow the dictates of reason, weigh carefully the advice of your solicitors, and reach a conclusion satisfactory to your business sense and your integrity.'

'Yes. Who is it from?'

'It is fading. I am sorry.'

Bill had a good view of the group around the table, from his wife's profile to the unobscured face of Mrs. Clayton, and it was mostly on this face that he fixed his eyes. The young woman from Barnet was watching Myra closely, with an expression of curiosity, fear and hope. Bill could see that she was probably younger than he'd at first supposed; it was the lines and darkness of worry and sleeplessness around her eyes and the tense set of the mouth that aged her.

He looked back to Myra as she began to speak again, and listened. She wasn't entranced, he knew by the sound of her voice, and he was interested in how she would satisfy her clients and make them happy by saying the most commonplace things. She was talking about a man, with a description that would have fitted ninety-five men out of a hundred, and the woman sitting next to Mrs. Clayton kept saying, 'Yes, that's Fred. That's my Fred,' and, 'Ask him about Mrs. Brown's Marion.' Myra dodged around every leading question, and finished with the woman by pronouncing, 'Take good care. Take good care.'

It was Mrs. Clayton's turn next, and Bill tensed. There was a moment of silence before he heard Myra say, 'You are worried about a child.'

'Yes.' The young woman's voice came loud and clear.

'You are worried because for the second time she has not come home when expected.'

'That's right.'

'You must be of good heart. Your child is safe. She is being taken care of by three people. They are not evil people, but . . .'

A noise intruded on Bill's hearing, a rustling noise from behind, and he swung his head quickly.

Adriana was getting off the bed.

Before he could move the picture down over the peephole she had trotted to his side and was standing staring up at him. She opened her mouth to speak, but he grabbed her arm, pulled her close and clamped a hand on her lips. She began to struggle and squirm and shake her head from side to side.

Mrs. Clayton's voice came through plainly: 'When will I get her back?'

Adriana froze, and Bill with her. Then the child suddenly burst into violent contortions, flailing and kicking. The noise of their movements seemed monstrously loud to Bill, and he darted a fearful glance at the peep-hole; but he dare not loose her to close it for fear she shouted the moment his hand left her mouth.

He used all his strength against her, lifting her bodily off the floor and clamping the back of her head to his chest. Slowly, and with a slight feeling of exhilaration at his superiority, he began to get the better of the fight. He imprisoned both her arms in his left one, and after taking two painful kicks on the shins trapped her legs between his knees. She still struggled, but was too tightly held now to allow much movement. He curved his hand closer around her mouth as she began to make gurgling sounds, and stopped them. He quickly leaned to the wall and put his eye to the hole to see if the rumpus had been noticed by the women. As before, the medium was the centre of attraction in the séance room.

Myra said, 'She is in a place that is built of wood. It is warm and dry, and she is being well cared for. You must not fear for her safety.'

'Yes.'

'The three people are now better disposed toward the child than they were wont to be, and are treating her with courtesy. They seem to be happy about something. All is well.'

'Yes.'

Myra thought she had told Mrs. Clayton all she could, and ended with, 'There is nothing more, except that you will see your daughter soon. Very soon. Tomorrow. Yes, tomorrow for certain you will see your daughter.'

'Thank you. Thank you very much.'

Myra moved her head slightly, toward the woman on the far right, wanting to hurry along the meeting. She knew the woman to be concerned about her husband's affair with his secretary, and began to frame her opening sentence around 'a young woman with a romantic attachment'.

She was about to pronounce the first word, but stopped.

Her chest had suddenly started to ache. She took a deep breath and began again to speak, and again stopped. The pain was getting worse. It was as though her lungs were so full of air they were about to burst.

She became frightened, pulled her hands free, clutched them to her breast, opened her eyes and mouth and tried to breathe out. She couldn't. The pain spread with a jump to her throat. She was choking. Her heart thumped wildly, her lungs swelled steadily, her eyes bulged from their sockets, her head roared with frantic noise, and mad fear struck like a knife zipped up the spine.

She leapt to her feet and screamed.

Bill jerked convulsively. His hair suddenly felt as if it were alive with crawling things. He was so unnerved he was barely conscious of the child still clamped in his arms. He watched unblinking as Myra, her hands around her throat, swayed forward on to the table and crashed down to the floor.

There was a frenzied bustling and babbling as the women crowded round. The ceiling light was switched on. Mrs. Clayton, the only one still sitting, looked down worriedly. Then the movement and noise stopped, and there was an expectant silence. Bill heard his wife's voice.

She said, 'Dead.'

He took one step back from the peep-hole. He closed his eyes tightly. He was overpowered with a feeling of horror; black dripping horror. His lips, mouth, his whole lower jaw began to tremble. The moan that escaped him tuned up to a squeak at the end. As though he'd been stung on it, he pulled his hand from the girl's face and pressed it to his lips. Adriana's head fell to the side.

With his eyes still closed he loosed his left arm, and felt her sag away from him and land with a soft thud on the floor. He cringed forward from the waist, holding a hand to his bubbling stomach, and forced himself to open his eyes and look, but knowing before he did what he would see. He knew the child was dead.

Adriana was lying on her back, her arms spread and her legs twisted. Her face was dark, and there was a slight frown between her partly open eyes. Her hands were clenched into tight white-knuckled fists.

Bill's legs gave way, and he sank slowly to his knees beside her. He stared, stupefied with grief and dread, at the lifeless form, and reached out a hand that dangled like an empty glove and touched the smooth brow, and whispered, the words blurred with saliva, 'I'm sorry. I'm sorry.'

Myra had been lifted on to a chair. She felt quite normal, all pain gone, but a little dazed and worried by the attack she'd just had. She was wondering if it could be her heart.

Her vision was filled with women's faces, all wearing expressions of alarm, wonder and ill-disguised delight. She smiled faintly, and the faces moved back. One of the women said, 'I'll get you a glass of water, shall I?' Myra nodded, but then remembered the bathroom window, and said quickly, 'No. No thank you. I am quite all right now.'

Another woman, the one whom she had been about to address when stricken, leaned forward and asked, 'Who is it?'

Myra blinked. 'I beg your pardon?'

'Who is it that's dead?' You went out like a light, then said, "Dead". Who did you mean?'

'I do not know,' Myra murmured. She didn't know, and only vaguely recalled saying the word. She had no idea why, or where it had come from. She thought it must have been a reaction to the fear she'd felt while having the attack.

'I hope you will excuse me, ladies,' she said, rising. 'But I must cut short this evening's meeting. I do not feel very well.'

There was a hushed chorus of suitable replies, though nearly every face showed disappointment; disappointment, Myra knew, not so much at the termination of the séance as at the lack of psychic significance in the dramatic faint.

She snuffed out the candle and went to the door, and led the way downstairs. She noticed two of the women glancing surreptitiously at Mrs. Clayton, who had fallen to the rear, and she thought they had probably realized who she was, connecting the name and the talk of the missing child. They would tell the others, and all would remember the words, 'You will see your child tomorrow.' Myra was very pleased.

She opened the door and stood to one side of the sill, and shook hands and exchanged a brief word with each woman, who, before reaching the doorway, had deposited an envelope on the hat-stand shelf. Mrs. Clayton was last. She glanced at the shelf, brought a wallet from her pocket and asked, 'What shall I give, Mrs. Savage?'

'There is no set fee. Just whatever you think.'

The woman drew a crackling five-pound note from the wallet. 'Will this be all right?'

'It is more than generous, Mrs. Clayton,' Myra said, accepting the money. 'I hope I have earned it.'

'Oh I assure you, you have. I feel much better now. My husband didn't want me to come, said I should wait for Adriana. You see, we expected all day since noon to be phoned and told where to go and get her. But when six o'clock came and we hadn't had word, I took a chance and drove over here. I'd have gone mad waiting all night to hear from these people, but now I can rest easy. We'll have her back tomorrow . . . won't we?'

'I am sure of it. I will stake my reputation on it.'

Mrs. Clayton sighed, smiling.

Myra said, 'It was true then, what the paper said, you have paid someone a ransom.'

'Oh yes.'

'And did not the police try and apprehend these people?—when the money was handed over.'

'Oh no. Charlie didn't want to take any risks. He told the police about the ransom, but not where he was going to take it.'

'Well, perhaps that was the wisest thing.'

'Yes. However, they told us later, the police, that they'd followed Charlie when he went to town this morning. They saw the money change hands and I think they got a good look at the man, but they didn't try and catch him or anything. But they did try to follow him. He was very clever though, they said, and they lost him.'

Myra tutted. 'Too bad. But what about the chauffeur?'

'Oh, I'm sure that's a lot of nonsense. Charlie and I are convinced he's not connected with it at all. We've had Henry with us for years. He's a fine man.'

'Still, I do not suppose you are greatly interested in the criminals. You just want your little girl back.'

Mrs. Clayton nodded. 'Exactly.' She put out her hand. 'Well, thank you very, very much, Mrs. Savage. You've eased my mind a great deal, and my husband will be relieved, too, when I tell him what you said—even though he doesn't think much of this kind of thing.'

'He can not be blamed for that, when so many people consider spiritualism to be nonsense. But we know different, do we not, Mrs. Clayton?'

'We certainly do. Good night.'

'Good night.' Myra waited till the young woman had passed through the gateway before closing the door, and sighing with satisfaction. Everything was ready, she thought. Everything was perfect. The 'good look' the police had had at Bill was unimportant; his face was changed radically by the cap and in the plastic mac his body seemed a great deal bulkier.

She turned her face upward, and shouted, 'Bill!' There was no reply. The house was very still. She frowned and shouted again. Silence; a silence that was somehow ominous. She went to the foot of the stairs and climbed three steps and shouted once more. Getting no answer she trotted briskly up to the landing, and listened outside the bedroom door for a moment before opening it.

She stood and stared, and gasped. Bill was kneeling by the side of the bed, his forearms and head resting on it. In the centre of the bed was a motionless form, moulded perfectly by the thin sheet that covered it from head to foot.

'My God!' she said harshly. 'What have you done?'

Sitting on the edge of her chair Myra was feeding Adriana's clothes to the fire, the sputter and hiss of which competed with the clock's tick in providing the only sounds to the room. She had torn the small overcoat to pieces, seam by seam, and was now in the process of burning the last slice of sleeve. It was almost midnight.

Bill was sitting on the couch, staring vacantly into the shadow under the table. An occasional blink and a regularly twitching nerve at the side of his sagged-down lower lip were the only intimations that he lived.

A button flared briefly with green flame, and the sleeve was gone. Myra picked up the shoes, set them firmly atop the coals and patted them down with the poker, making a mental note to remember to search the ashes for the heavy metal buckles.

In the hours since the child's death Myra had rationalized herself from fear to calm. To begin with, the death itself was to her no tragedy; no death was to her a tragedy; almost the reverse. And the horror had been taken out of the affair by her husband's saying, mumbling, as he had been led meekly from the bedroom, that it was an accident. There was the worry of the consequences, now greatly multiplied, should they be found out, but she had confidence in herself and in her dream; they would not be found out. She was sorry for the parents, genuinely sorry; but the mother was young and would have more children. Apart from a slight change in arrangements everything would go as planned, and the primary result would be as planned—except that it would be better than originally anticipated; the story would now get international attention. The ultimate result was almost guaranteed.

She tapped at the shoes till they were hidden in the centre of the fire, and turned to look at her husband. She said, 'It is cold by the window. You had better come and sit in your chair.'

There was no response. She said sharply, 'Bill!'

He jerked his head round, blinking rapidly. 'Mmm?'

'Come and sit by the fire.'

He rose very slowly, and very slowly came to the hearth, bowing over his clasped hands and with his head angled a little to one side. Sitting well into the chair his body was stiff for a moment, then it began to sag.

Myra laid down the poker, and asked, 'How did it happen?'

It was a full minute before he answered, in a spiritless monotone, 'She fell off the bed.'

'Head first? It must have been.'

'Yes.'

'Then what?'

He gave a frowning wince.

She said, 'She just died?'

'Yes.'

'Instantly?'

'Yes.'

'Well. Well, she did not suffer at all. That is something, is it not?'

He made no reply. She glanced at him and went on, 'You

must not take this so hard. It could not be helped. I hope you are not going to blame yourself. Accidents will happen you know, anywhere. It could have happened just the same had she been at home. The fact that it happened here has no bearing on us. We cannot blame ourselves. We might just as well blame the salesman who sold us the bed, or the man who made it, or the Claytons for conceiving the child, or their parents for conceiving them, or ours for us.'

She glanced at him again, and saw that he'd probably not heard a word she'd said. His eyes were fixed dreamily on the smoke just above the fire. His legs were spread apart from the knees down, but the toes made contact again by sagging in and touching. His right hand was going through a routine: starting at the hairline, the forefinger and thumb came down one on either side of the brow, moved inward along the eybrows, met and went together down the nose, separated to skirt the nostrils, wiped out the corners of the mouth, briefly plucked forward the bottom lip, slid over the chin, down the throat, circled the tie to its point, caressed the wrist of the other lap-lying hand for a moment, and rose slowly to the brow to repeat the circuit.

Myra said, 'Children die every day, in all manner of horrible ways. And you must remember, she is far happier now than she has ever been, or ever would be in this life. I envy her.'

He made no sign to acknowledge what she had said. She went on, 'I know this sounds awful, but really you know, we are a lot safer now that she will be unable to talk about her abduction. I did not mention it before, but it occurred to me that she would be sure to mention the white furniture, and since it has already been seen by that detective it would not help us at all if we removed the paint. But apart from anything like that, if the police were suspicious that we were involved, they need only bring the girl back here and she would recognize me. There are many reasons for our being better off by this development.'

Seeing there was still no reaction to her words, she gave up the attempt to console and became brisk. 'Well,' she said, 'now we must needs make a change or two in the plans. You *are* listening to me, are you not?'

'Yes,' he said softly, his hand just leaving his mouth. 'Yes.'

'Early in the morning you will take the child away. Not to the hut you had selected, but somewhere else. I think Epping Forest. You will leave her near some sort of landmark, and when you come home I will go and telephone the Claytons and the police and the newspapers, and describe the place where you have left the child. The next day you can take the money and leave it at the hut, and I will do some more phoning. You understand? You agree?'

He nodded.

'Good.' She rose and moved between the chairs. 'We must turn in now and get some sleep. It will be a busy morning.' She left the room, and reappeared a minute later with her arms full of blankets. She made up the bed on the couch, quickly and roughly, and returned to the hearth. Bending down she touched her husband's hand, shuddering at the coldness of it, and said, 'Please try to sleep. This is an awful thing that has happened, but do not blame yourself. Try and be logical about it. Good night.' She patted the hand, and turned and left the room.

Bill hardly noticed her leaving, had hardly noticed her presence, and had only vaguely been aware of her speaking. His state of mind had not changed even slightly since the child's death. He was still stunned with grief, a grief felt as deeply for the death itself as it was for his causing it. Far from being logical or doing any ratiocinating, his mind had not moved away from the act of dying, not even to consider the magnitude of it, as crime; he felt only moral guilt.

So stunned was he that he didn't know his head ached or his limp arm throbbed with rheumatic pain or that his breathing was difficult. He gazed at the smoke-curtained black back of the fireplace and saw, and saw over and over, the scene in the bedroom, and suffered torments. Occasionally he broke the pattern by thinking dully of what might have been had he not done such and such a thing or if the child had not tried to do so and so; but these breaks were fleeting, since the ifs and buts proved more agonizing than the facts.

He lost all sense of time. He didn't see the fire fade, flicker and die, or feel the cold air come cuddling close.

But it was, finally, the cold and his pains and the squeaking effort of breathing that roused him. He sat forward, looked dazedly at the ugly grey ruin in the grate, shivered, and rose and moved across to his bed.

After undressing mechanically, and just as mechanically folding his clothes with his usual neatness, he walked slowly around the table a dozen times, bending over his tightly clenched hands. He stopped by the sideboard and pulled open a drawer, and looked for the child's clothes. When he didn't find them he closed the drawer carefully and went into the kitchen. He was shivering so hard that the carrier bag rattled as he brought it from the cupboard and carried it to the table. He took out the oranges, setting them on their tops so they wouldn't roll, and his cap and macintosh, and lifted out the blue bag. The white package was tied on, and without haste he unfastened each of the many knots. Unfolding the wrappings, he found inside a thick wad of banknotes and a piece of paper. Written in pencil on the paper was, *It would not all go in the bag. Please don't hurt my baby.*

His throat constricted, and convulsively he clapped the paper to his eyes and cried into it.

Four

THE DAYLIGHT HAD REACHED ITS FULL STRENGTH, which was a dull greyness that gave a firm promise of rain. The lounge curtains were still pulled to, but they were so flimsy and skimped that the room was very little darker than it would have been were they drawn back.

Bill was standing by the table. He was dressed, and wearing his coat, helmet, goggles and gloves, and Myra was tucking the scarf in around his neck. She gave it a final pat, stood back and said, 'There you are. All right?'

His head dipped forward gently in a nod; the rest of his body remained motionless.

'Right. Now you just sit down for a minute. I will see to everything.' She turned and left the room, stepped out of the house briefly to open the screening half of the garage door, came back in and took the stairs rapidly in short chopping steps. There was no time to be wasted, she thought; it was already eight-thirty and there was a lot to do; things that should have been done and finished with for an hour or more, and would have been had she not slept in.

She entered the back bedroom and switched on the light. The sheet-covered form was just as she had last seen it the night before, and looking at it as she approached she reflected on how much death belied the truth; it denoted end and decay, when it was actually a vivid beginning. She stood at the side of the bed, leaned over and tilted the body toward her, tucking the sheet behind it, then did the same at the near side and at the head and feet. Noticing the flash of something black on a corner of the sheet as it was flicked through the air, she caught at it and saw that it was stamped with a laundry mark. She hurriedly fetched a pair of nail-scissors from her room and cut away the smudgy black letters.

She lifted the body, surprised that it stayed so neat and straight, and left the room with it held across her breast. Going outside the back way she walked briskly round to the garage. The side-car was open and ready. She slid the long white bundle inside, then secured the cover.

Back in the lounge, panting a little from her haste, she said, 'Now, you know what you have to do?'

Bill was still standing where she'd left him. He said, 'Yes.'

She thought that since she had just spent fifteen minutes going over everything she'd said the night before, he would have to be very far gone with grief and worry not to know what he had to do. She said, 'Right. Just make sure it is a place that can be recognized from a description. An unusual rock formation or clump of flowers for instance. Or a particularly large tree. And of course in a fairly pin-pointable section of the forest. Understand?'

'Yes.'

'Right. Come along.' She led the way outside and stood by the garage door as he went in. She watched him start the engine, and took a step back from the noise.

A hand touched her shoulder.

She gasped, and shuddered round quickly. The delivery boy was standing there, holding out the newspaper and smiling. She drew a deep breath and glared the smile off his face, and took the paper abruptly. He backed away, blinking, and turned suddenly, grabbed his gatepost-leant bicycle and pushed off. She cursed him under her breath.

As Bill drove out of the garage she hid the newspaper behind her, hoping he wouldn't see it; she didn't want any delay in his leaving. But he didn't appear to see even her. He went by without turning his head, eased down on to the road and set off up the street.

Myra watched him, frowning. She wasn't happy about the state of his mind. She knew he had gone to pieces because of the girl's death, but wasn't sure to what extent he'd let himself go. She shook her head, and hoped he would keep his wits about him.

Going into the house she stood in the hall to look at the newspaper. The headline blared WHERE IS LITTLE ADRIANA? Myra quickly skimmed through the story. Essentially it was the same as the evening before, except for the new angle of the parents waiting for the ransomed child. There was a picture of Charles Clayton, grim-faced, walking through his gateway, but the other pictures were the same, and the chauffeur was still assisting the police.

Myra felt a slight disappointment. She had expected, for no particular reason, to find something along the lines of, *Last night Mrs. Clayton drove to north-east London to attend a séance at the home of Mrs. Myra Savage, a well-known medium, and was told* . . . She sighed and threw the paper on the hatstand shelf.

About to move away, she stopped and frowned, then raised her eyebrows and smiled quietly. She had remembered her words at the séance; remembered that she had said the child would be found today, and that was all, with no mention of whether she'd be alive or dead. She would be found today. The prediction was still good, and the others at the séance would remember it, and possibly—and Myra's smile widened—remember and connect the word *Dead* with the prediction.

The smile went as her lower jaw dropped. She had suddenly realized, for the first time, that what had made her pronounce the word was a clear case of precognition, that the attack, which had cost her hours of sleepless worry, was in fact the moment of dying, experienced simultaneously with the child. It was the most powerful and immediate of all the phenomena she had ever produced.

A thrill ran through her, and she stood quite still for five minutes, relishing her achievement.

Rubbing her hands together she went along the hall and into the kitchen, and quickly set to work. The bag of money and the half-wrapped wad of notes were put in the pantry, and the oranges were carried into the lounge and laid in the table's fruit-bowl. She looked around, thinking she would do the other jobs in rotation of importance: sift the ashes, light the fire to burn the plastic macintosh, carrier bag and blue cap, remove the boards from the upstairs windows, empty the rest of the chloroform down the toilet and break the bottle in the field behind the back garden, and wipe everything within a child's reach in the bedroom and bathroom.

From Josephine Avenue to Epping Forest was but a fifteen-minute journey, and Bill was driving at a steady unhurried pace, a pace that belied his feelings and mental processes. Unlike the dull one-track sorrow it was weighted with the night before, his mind was now as confused and full of flitting thought as a fever dream. Mixed surrealistically with the thoughts—themselves almost spoken words, running through his head as if on ticker-tape—were vivid and frighteningly true pictures; pictures of himself being brutally questioned by police, being thrown in dark cells, standing pleading in a hostile courtroom, and repeatedly being hanged. The scene of the child's death came and went frequently; but whereas before the words accompanying it revolved around Tragedy, now they revolved around Murder. He knew there was no doubt as to what the death would be considered: a smothering: a murder; and in the picture of himself in the prisoner's box, the explanation he gave of how it had happened was so feeble that it would have been hilarious were it not for the hanging scene that followed close upon it. His pity was felt now more for himself than for the child, and he knew he would have to stop at nothing in preventing his connexion with the death being discovered. There was no question of right or wrong, moral or legal; there was only the all-consuming concern for self.

He suddenly braked, recognizing a street on his immediate left as the one he wanted to take, and was just able to turn into it, albeit on the wrong side of the road. As he steered across to the correct side he saw a policeman ahead, walking slowly and pushing a bicycle, and he got a strong urge to stop by him, kneel at his feet and confess everything. The urge was so powerful that he clenched his teeth and trembled, afraid of what he might do. But he passed the policeman safely.

The houses on the street changed from fairly large to small to well-spaced cottages. With the cottages the road became gravel, and after a few hundred yards it narrowed into a cinder lane and began to curve and wind.

He had been on this semi-unknown route to the forest several times, for Sunday picnics, and was quite familiar with it, but due to his present mental state it was five minutes before he realized he had passed the cut-off he should have taken. The lane was barely wide enough for the machine to turn in, but he managed it without reversing.

He drove back and turned off through a gateway, on to a track that had a belt of high grass running down the centre. On one side, beyond a small fragile hedgerow, was a rubbish dump that covered several acres, an ugly mess of old tyres, oil drums, odd-shaped chunks of metal and sodden cartons lying about among piles of smaller garbage. Standing near a pyramid of paint cans was a man, leaning on a shovel and looking down at a fire that smouldered at his feet. At the sound of the motor-cycle he turned his head, stared for a moment, and looked away.

The track rose and fell and twisted, and finally came to an end in a small paddock surrounded on three sides by tall dense hedges profusely covered with bramble. On the fourth side was a barbed wire fence, and a yard behind it the trees of Epping Forest.

Bill drove around the paddock and came to a stop beside the wire and with his machine facing the exit. He switched off the ignition and sat for a moment listening. It was quiet, with only faint and scattered bird-calls. He got to the ground and quickly opened the side-car cover, keeping his face averted. With his eyes fixed on the hedge he felt down and grasped the sheeted body. The first contact of his hands made him shudder, but he forced himself to go on, and lifting out the long bundle he held it across his waist.

He had no trouble with the fence. There were only two strands of wire, and he trod on the bottom one and slid under the top. He went forward into the trees, walking in as close to a straight line as he could; he didn't want to get confused and be unable to find his way back.

Almost at once the body began weighing heavily on his arms. The load would have been eased considerably were he to lift it close to his chest, but he preferred to keep it at a full-arm distance, and even tried to ignore the fact that he had it.

When he'd penetrated so far that on glancing back he was unable to see the light at the edge of the forest, he began looking for a suitable place to leave the body; looking carelessly, not intending to waste too much time seeking perfection.

A peculiarly shaped bush caught his eye, and he stopped and looked at it; but he soon saw with regret that it wasn't peculiar enough—there was another identical with it a little way ahead, and another beyond that.

He was about to move on when he heard a faint crackle coming from somewhere on the right. He froze, leaning forward, and listened intently. There was silence, then, clearly, a voice. It cried, 'Reg! This way!'

He moved quickly, heading to the left, heading away from the caller, whom he judged to be about fifty feet away. The trees had become close set, making for better cover, but making speed difficult—he had to turn with practically every stride.

A fallen tree lay across his path. He was lifting his leg over it when he realized it would make the perfect landmark. He turned right and walked along beside the trunk, which got thicker by degrees and rose till it was shoulder high and ended in a massive spread of red roots that he had to detour two yards to circle.

The base of the tree was at the edge of a small clearing, and he moved into the centre of it and looked all round before turning back to the jagged crater the tree had left behind.

'Hey, Reg!'

Bill jumped. The caller seemed right at his back. The bundle fell from his arms as he whirled around, and a bare leg flopped out of the sheet.

There was no one in sight, but sounds of passage were very

close. He turned and ran to the edge of the clearing. Another shout came from behind; he didn't catch the words but it spurred him on.

He reached the trees and had to reduce his run to a striding walk, and began to twist and turn, weaving between the trunks as quickly as possible, yet not quickly enough to keep up to the speed of his heart.

Suddenly the trees were widely spaced and he was able to run again, and he ran as hard as he could. The goggles started to bounce on his nose, and he held them in place with one hand. There were more shouts from behind, but he wasn't sure how far behind, and he wasn't going to stop and listen and find out.

He saw a wide stream on his left, and moved to its bank and ran along beside it. A moment later he saw another stream on his right, running parallel to the first one and drawing in towards it up ahead. Before he had realized the strangeness of this he was brought to a halt.

The streams met in front of him and became a large body of water, and he saw immediately that it was not two streams, or one, but a crescent-shaped pond, and that he was at the point of the peninsula. He would have to go back.

He turned, took one step, and stopped. Three boys were coming in a half run towards him. They had dirty faces, were aged about twelve, and wore untidy Scout uniforms. One shouted, 'Hey, mister!'

Bill was so frightened that for a moment he couldn't move. Then he did move, in the only way open to him: in the boys' direction. He veered to the right, keeping close to the edge of the water, and tried to run, but could get his legs to perform merely a jerky walk.

The boys clustered together and stopped in his path. Their faces were vacant with excitement. One spread his arms and said, 'Hey, mister.'

Bill tried to skirt round them, but they moved in a body to front him again. He said, 'Go 'way.'

They all began speaking at once, their voices high and breathless: 'Mister, come quick. We've found a dead corpse.' 'It's true, mister. Honest.' 'I saw it first.'

He pushed through them roughly, treading on a toe. 'Go 'way.'

One grabbed his sleeve. 'It's over 'ere by a big tree. It's a dead corpse.'

'No, no!' Bill gasped, shaking off the hand. '*Please.*'

Another ran ahead and stood in his path, and jerked a thumb to the side. 'You're goin' the wrong way, mister. Come on. It's in a sheet. I saw it first.'

'Leave me alone,' Bill said, and shoved the boy aside and stumbled on. The interference stopped, and there was silence from behind. Then he heard the boys shout, in unison, as though at the sight of someone:

'Oh, Mr. Benson. Come quick!'

And now Bill was suddenly able to run. He ran madly, wildly, skimming dangerously close to trees and crashing through low branches, throwing his arms and legs out without rhythm, changing their strokes from short to long and back again, despairing at the way his coat pulled at his thighs and petrified by a new fear: his lungs were tightening swiftly, as though being pressed together. He knew he was about to have an attack of asthma.

Now he could hear the thud of running feet from behind, and not too far behind. Then a deep, adult voice shouted, 'Hey, you! Stop!'

He ran on, careless of direction, taking the clearest way that presented itself, veering left a few yards, right a few yards and sometimes almost doubling on his tracks to avoid a closely set clump of trees.

He came on to a narrow path that went in a clear straight line, and ran even faster. The footfalls from the rear now seemed very close. Suddenly there was a bush in front of him. He was going too fast to stop or turn or do anything but jump. He jumped, throwing up his arms and lifting his forward leg high.

The leg wasn't high enough. His foot caught in the bush and he shot over it head first. He landed with a crash on his stomach and elbows and knees, and his head jerked as the helmet slammed against the base of a tree.

The asthma that had been creeping up slowly now swooped its relentless clutch on to his lungs, and he drew in a shuddering, screeching breath. He lay perfectly still for a second, then scrambled frantically but weakly to his feet.

He tried to start running even before he was fully erect and he trod on the front of his coat and pitched forward again on to his face. The sound of rapid footsteps thudded into his ears from the ground below him.

He got up quickly, icy with fear, and took a few half-running strides. He stopped, grabbed hold of a tree and clung to it, and began fighting madly to get air into his lungs. The asthma had reached its full strength; he was being strangled.

He could hear nothing now other than the screech and whine from his windpipe. He pulled his mouth far back at the sides, rolled his eyes to the sky, and struggled. His trembling legs sagged under him as he turned all his energy on the fight for air, and his upper body swung slowly round the trunk of the tree till he was facing the way he had come.

A hatless man, young and hefty and wearing the short pants of the Scout uniform, was running forward and just about to jump over the bush six feet away.

Bill didn't care. He didn't care about anything. All he wanted to do was breathe. He'd just got his lungs full and was starting on the eye-bulging effort of emptying them. He clenched his fists, hunched his shoulders, squeezed the tree and forced up his diaphragm. Every muscle in his body, especially those in his stomach, threw themselves into the job. A thousand hot needles drove into his chest.

The young man landed from his leap over the bush, staggered, recovered, and came quickly forward. He looked scared but determined, his thick-lipped mouth severely set. Reaching Bill's side he hesitated, then suddenly grabbed an arm and pulled it toward him.

Bill's grip on the tree was broken. He hadn't the strength to hold himself up with one hand. He sagged down and fell over on to his back, and lay there staring at the young man, who'd got to one knee beside him, trying to say with his eyes what it was impossible for him to spare the air to put into words; trying to say that he would do anything, confess anything, sell his soul, just so long as he was left alone to breathe.

It was twice as hard for his lungs to function now that he was lying flat, and he clawed weakly at the hand on his arm and tried to pull himself up by it.

The faint touch of fear had gone from the young man's face; it was confident, almost smugly so. He put both hands on Bill's shoulders, swung a leg across his body and kept him pressed firmly to the ground. Turning his head up and to the side he gave a loud shout.

To Bill it was like a terrible nightmare. It was like drowning in a small glass tank that was surrounded by laughing spectators. He knew he was dying, and quickly. His only hope was to sit up. He flapped his fists uselessly and with a horrible sluggishness against his killer's face, which he saw merely as a pink blur, obscured by tears and the partly steamed goggles. The young man didn't even bother to dodge the poor blows.

Bill's mouth was wide open. The frantic screech of his windpipe and the high-pitched wail that now went with it sounded like the top notes of an accordion, but to him amplified tenfold. It was the only thing he could hear. It was as though he were listening to his own requiem.

His heart began to strike tremendous thuds against his pain-slashed lungs. He was seized with a paroxysm; his arms stiffened and his knees shot up.

The young man disappeared, and Bill was suddenly free. Using only his stomach muscles and the force of his will he swung into a sitting position. He put his hands behind to support himself, closed his eyes in an agony of relief, and went on with the only slightly eased struggle for air.

He opened his eyes again, and saw the young man, both hands clasped to his crotch, rolling around and grovelling his face into the grass in a madness of pain.

With the slight abatement of his agony, Bill turned his mind to the danger of the situation; but he wasn't sure that he could do anything about it. He was torn between staying and breathing and being caught, and leaving. Leaving meant taking some of the effort away from the working of his lungs and using it to walk with; if he could walk; if he could move. He decided to try, but slowly, and to stop at once if his breathing became too greatly affected.

He carefully swung forward and over, over on to his hands and knees, and crawled along a few feet in slow motion. He thought of his motor-cycle, and what it was like driving on it, with his mouth open to the rush of air. He began to crawl faster, at something like the pace of a steady stroll.

He heard voices, calling, 'Mr. Benson! Mr. Benson!' and glanced back. There was no one in sight, other than the young man still rolling in silent agony on the ground.

He began to crawl faster yet, his impetus caused as much by the thoughts of the wind on the speeding bike as by his imminent capture. He stopped by a tree, grasped it and pulled himself slowly erect. With hands out at either side and head down he started to walk, sinking low as his legs bent shakily every time they took on the full weight of his body.

The trees became closely set again and he was able to help himself along from one to another. He heard more shouts, though only faintly above the noise of his breathing, and he couldn't judge how far back they were. He turned his head, but saw no farther than the fourth or fifth tree.

He went another two yards, then stopped and lifted the goggles and wearily wiped his eyes. The pain in his chest was crippling, and so were the pains across his shoulders and in his quiveringly taut abdomen and at the small of his back. He knew he could relieve all but the chest pains by sitting down, and he had nearly decided to do that when he heard the voices again.

There was an unintelligible shout from a youngster, then a clear gruff one: 'You try that way. You that way. I'll go up there. And you, Reg, you go for the police. And don't forget . . .' The rest of it was lost to his ears as he turned and walked on. He went as fast as he dare; he wanted to run, but was afraid he'd strangle.

He didn't know for sure that he was heading in the right direction. His mind wasn't capable of working out in reverse all the twists and turns he'd made on entering and being chased. He just pressed forward, and thought that at least he was going away from those behind; and that was something.

Then he saw sky thinly striped between the trees on his right, and turned. After a dozen steps the trees ended, and he was standing beside the barbed wire fence. Ahead were fields and distant houses, and the forest curved back out of sight at either side. There was no sign of the paddock, and the bike.

He eased slowly through the wire, hesitated, and took a gamble and turned right, keeping close to the fence, walking like an old man, each step a separate project. He heard someone crashing through the trees close by, but didn't change his speed.

Around the curve of the forest he saw, jutting out, a thorn hedge. It lengthened as he approached, and he realized with a thrill of relief that it was the wall of the paddock. He thought of speeding along on the bike, with the air being forced down his throat, and, even better, his atomizer waiting at home to give him immediate ease.

As he neared the hedge he saw that it formed the back of the paddock; the opening was round the far side; there would be a fifty-yard journey to get to it. He was despairing at the thoughts of the impossible distance, wondering how he would ever cover it, when he noticed that all he had to do was get back under the wire again. He did so, slowly, and walked along the edge of the forest till he was past the hedge. His old machine was waiting for him, and he felt a sudden surge of affection for it; the emotion was so strong that his eyes moistened.

He crawled through the wire and moved shakily to the bike. Switching on the ignition, he pulled down the starter pedal and tried to kick it. He didn't have the strength.

His body sagged and he gazed sadly at the engine, and listened dreamily as a long lingering shout came from among the trees. He tried the pedal again, but couldn't get it down beyond the first loose inch. His eyes closed and for a moment he gave way to his suffering, folding his arms across his agonized chest and moaning. He felt like sobbing, but he knew it would interfere too much with his breath and he would be liable to choke.

The thought of his atomizer forced him to take hold of himself, and think. He glared at the pedal, and immediately got an idea. He put his left foot on it, sank down on his right leg, then jerked his body up into the air. The full weight of him came down on the pedal and it shot toward the ground. The engine roared into life and Bill fell over on to his back.

He got up slowly, on the verge of giving way again, and swung wearily into the saddle. There was a slight relief for his lungs as he leaned forward on the handlebars, and more when he revved and moved off and a breeze began to flow by.

He went out of the paddock and put on speed and soon he was travelling rockily along the overgrown track at forty miles an hour. At the last bend before going out of sight of the forest he glanced behind; there was no one to be seen at the edge of the trees. He passed the rubbish dump, now untended, and turned on to the cinder lane.

Just before reaching the gravel a car came towards him, and he had to slow and move close to the side. He looked warily at the driver, a woman, but she was too occupied with steering through the limited space to pay him much attention.

He accelerated, rattled noisily over the gravel, came to the tarmac and accelerated still more. At the end of the road he swung without slowing on to the highway and began to weave quickly around the traffic, careless of the fact that he was exceeding the legal limit.

Less than ten minutes later he turned into Josephine Avenue. He fixed his eyes on the large red and white *For Sale* poster in the window of the house next to his, and thought hungrily of the atomizer waiting just beyond. He bounced down the long road and drove straight into his garage, stopping with a squealing jerk that nearly pitched him over the handlebars.

The front door opened as he was reaching for the knocker. He brushed by his wife, went into the lounge, flung his gloves aside, pulled out a drawer in the side-board, grabbed his atomizer, took the stopper from the glass spout, put the spout in his mouth and began rapidly to squeeze the rubber bulb. The bitter but joyfully welcome taste of the drug filled his mouth as the spray spread and was drawn into his windpipe. He closed his eyes and whimpered.

Almost at once his breathing was easier and its noise reduced to half-volume. He took the pump from his mouth and cuddled it against his neck, and raised the other hand to unfasten the helmet strap. Aided by his wife he removed his things, then went to his chair and sank gratefully into it. Another session of squeezing with the atomizer, and he had enough breath to spare to speak. He looked up at his wife, who was standing watching him anxiously, and gave her a weak smile.

She asked, 'Feel better?'

'Yes.'

'That was a bad attack.'

'Terrible . . . thought I'd die.'

'Did it just come on now?'

'No . . . long time ago . . . in Epping.'

'In the woods?'

'Yes.'

'What happened? Everything is all right, is it not?'

'Well . . .'

She frowned and folded her arms. 'Tell me everything.'

He drew in a deep breath, and spoke as he let it out: 'I'd just picked out a place to leave her when these Boy Scouts came flying through the trees and I had to . . .' He paused to draw in air, then went on, 'And I had to drop her and run.'

Myra's arms fell to her sides. 'What?'

'I had . . .'

'You mean someone saw you? You mean the body has been found?'

'Well, they saw me, yes, but with the helmet and . . .'

'Never mind that,' she cut in. 'Has the body been found?'

'Well, yes.'

She turned away, flapping her arms despairingly and raising her face to the ceiling. 'My God. All for nothing. All that for absolutely nothing. Already found. My God.'

'It was these Scouts,' he said lamely. 'You know.'

She suddenly broke from her abject attitude and quickly circled the table to the door. 'There might be time to tell the Claytons before they are notified. There just might.' She swung around. 'Quick now. Describe the place.'

'Oh, well, there's a fallen tree, a long one, with big red roots.'

'And where is she exactly?'

'Right by the roots.'

'And where is the tree exactly? What part of the forest?'

'Um, north-west corner. About twenty yards in.'

He heard her leave the room, thud quickly upstairs, slam a

door and thud down again. She appeared beside his chair, her face flushed, buttoning on her overcoat. She said, 'North-west corner. Fallen tree with red roots. Anything else?'

'No, I don't think so.'

'What kind of a tree was it?'

'I don't know. But it was longer than the others around it. Oh, and about a quarter of a . . . of a mile from that side of the forest there's a big rubbish dump.'

'Rubbish dump. Right. And how long ago was all this?'

'About half an hour.'

She nodded and turned away abruptly.

He heard the front door open, then slam. He sighed and settled himself and closed his eyes. He wasn't too perturbed by the situation; at the moment all worries and problems were relegated to second place; his mind was mainly concerned with the marvel of being able to draw breath.

Myra hurried along the street, with head down and hands thrust angrily into her coat pockets. She seethed as she considered the mess her husband had made of everything.

First, she thought, he allows the child to kill herself, putting them both in grave danger, then he more or less hands the body over to the authorities. It was intolerable and ruinous. The main part of the scheme, the part that would have accomplished most, had fizzled out into nothing. There was not really a great deal to be gained by telephoning the Claytons; it was just that a modicum of profit might be salvaged from the fiasco, and if nothing else it would keep the supernormal element in their minds and make the money-bag dream immediately acceptable.

That, the money, she thought consolingly, was the only thing that saved the affair from being a total and absolute failure. But it would cause no sensation, even if it worked out perfectly; the newspapers would be concentrating on the child's death and the hue and cry for what was assumed to be a murderer, and shove the less dramatic monetary angle to a quiet corner. Even so, every last particle of value would have to be got out of the finding of the ransom; nothing must be neglected, no detail. And to do that it would be better to delay it for a few days; let the case simmer on the discovery of the body. Then, after leaving the bag in the builder's hut, not only would the Claytons, the newspapers and the police be told where it could be found, but also, and perhaps preferably first, the Society for Psychical Research. The description of the hut could be made fairly vague, or at least the district it lay in could, so that there would be as long a delay as possible between the telling of the dream and the finding of the money. And perhaps a few articles of clothing could be left with the bag, apparent clues to the kidnappers; that would make the papers more interested.

There was still a good chance, she thought, that partly ruined as it was, the Plan could yet prove successful.

She reached the end of the street and turned right. Just ahead on the opposite side of the road was a phone kiosk. She had started to cross over to it when the idea came to her that it might be useful to have a witness to the telephone conversation. She turned back to the pavement and quickened her step. Mrs. Finch, one of her clients and an ardent admirer, lived in the next street but one.

After a swiftly covered hundred yards she turned a corner, and turned again through a gateway in front of a house that was identical with her own. She rapped hard on one of the glass panes in the door, then frowned fretfully at the silence that followed.

The frown went at the sound of a bang from the rear of the house, and she tapped one foot impatiently. The door opened and a woman smiled out at her. Myra said, 'Hello, Mrs. Finch.'

Mrs. Finch was about sixty-five, and very thin. Her sharp-edged features were thickly coated with pure white face powder, and on each cheekbone was a perfectly circular blob of bright orange rouge. Her dress was purple. She said, with a fluttering eagerness, 'Well of all *things*. Mrs. Savage. *Please* come in.'

Myra stepped inside. 'I am sorry to burst in on you like this, but I have to make a telephone call of the greatest import.' She gestured toward the phone that was perched on the gas-meter cupboard. 'Would I be inconveniencing you . . .?'

Mrs. Finch was aghast. 'Oh *no*. Not at *all*. You're very welcome I'm *sure*. But you will stop and have a cup of tea, won't you? Oh, of *course* you will.'

Myra moved round to the telephone. 'Well, I can only stay a minute or two.'

'I'll put the kettle on right away,' the woman said, closing the door quickly. 'It'll be ready in no time.' She turned and hurried down the hall with her arms raised and waving ring-throttled fingers in the air close to her head.

Myra lifted the receiver and carefully dialled. She heard

the call signal, and glanced over her shoulder, and was pleased to see that the kitchen door was ajar. The phone clicked and a female voice said, 'The Clayton residence.'

'I would like to speak to either Mr. or Mrs. Clayton, if you please. This is Myra Savage calling.'

'Yes. Would you please hold on.'

There was a short silence before a gruff voice said, 'Good morning, Mrs. Savage. Charles Clayton speaking.'

'Good morning. I do not know how you will respond to what I have to say, Mr. Clayton, since you did not seem to be very interested in my gifts the last time we spoke together. And . . .'

'Mrs. Savage,' the man said impatiently. 'I'm afraid I must ask you to please come to the point. We're expecting, or at least hoping for, an important phone call.'

Myra thought that Clayton's voice wasn't as strong and vibrant as when she had seen him in Barnet; it had a new, hurried weakness about it and the diction was poor. She said, 'Very good. This morning I had what I call a vision, a sort of waking dream.'

Clayton sighed, and said, 'Yes?'

'It concerned your daughter. I think I know where she can be found.'

'Yes.' The voice didn't sound too impressed.

'She is surrounded by trees, many many trees, and is close to one that is lying on the ground uprooted. This tree is very long and its roots are reddish. I am sure she is in danger. She is dressed in a long white gown that is far too large for her. She is lying quite still and probably sleeping. I did not actually see her, I just sensed she was there. All I saw was the white gown and the red roots of the tree. And I felt there were several people moving around her, some of them quite young, almost children.'

'Well, what precisely does all this mean, Mrs. Savage?'

'Much of it may be symbolic, such as the colour of the roots, meaning danger, but I am sure that the large number of trees can be taken as actual. I also got the impression that close by there was a collection of waste, refuse. I do not know what that signifies, but perhaps it will help narrow the search for the right spot. I would suggest you try Burnham Beeches. It is more or less on your side of London.'

Clayton sighed. 'I can't see how this helps me. I can't go tearing off to every wooded area around the city.'

'You could simply tell the police. They will check.'

'Oh, really now, Mrs. Savage. How could I possibly tell the police a story like that.'

'I really think you ought to. After all, you know, there is . . .'

'Mrs. Savage,' he cut in. 'I'm very sorry, but I'm afraid I'll have to ring off now. I want to keep the line free.'

'I would like to speak to your wife,' Myra said, making her tone stern.

'My wife's resting. I'm sorry. Good day.'

'But I think you are being . . .'

'Good day.' The phone went dead.

Myra shrugged, and smiled faintly as she put the receiver down. She thought that at least she had been able to get to Clayton before he was told of his child's death; it was better than nothing, and in future he would not be so sceptical. She put the receiver back to her face and dialled the other number she had memorized; the number of a national newspaper. She got a busy signal, and dialled again, changing the last digit. A male voice said, 'Good morning. *Daily Star.*'

Myra said, 'I would like to talk to someone who is connected with the Clayton kidnapping.'

'Oh, is it about the body in Epping Forest?'

Myra hesitated, then said, 'Yes. That is right.'

'Well, thanks all the same, but we already know. We've had several calls about it. Our men are on their way there now. But we don't know yet for sure that it is the Clayton girl. Do you know for sure?'

Myra said, 'No, not really.' She decided there was no point in telling the story of the vision.

'Okay. Thanks for calling. 'Bye.'

'Good day.' She set the receiver back in its cradle, and turned and called, 'Mrs. Finch!'

The kitchen door swung open at once and the woman's white face looked out. 'Oh, are you finished?'

'Yes, thank you. But I just want to ring the exchange and find out how much I owe you for the calls.'

'Oh *please*, my dear. I wouldn't *dream.*' She wafted the air, as though pushing the idea away. 'Now come into the kitchen. The kettle's almost boiling.'

'Well,' Myra said, walking down the hall, 'one of the calls might be quite expensive. It was to Barnet. To the Claytons, you know. About their little girl who was kidnapped.'

'*No!*'

* * *

Bill had tucked his atomizer safely down beside the deep seat-cushion of his chair, and was now dozing lightly, a faint smile on his lips and a worried slant to his eyebrows. His breathing was slow and measured, and sometimes his head quivered at the end of an inhale, but it was accompanied by only one thin squeak.

A sound broke gradually into his dreamless doze, and stopped just as he came fully awake. He blinked widely, trying to think what the noise had been. Then his mouth twisted in a little yawn and he closed his eyes again. Slowly the worried slant of his eyebrows deepened into a severe frown, and he opened his eyes and stared at the man-telshelf.

Not having to think too much about his breathing now, his mind had returned to his troubles and he was sinking quickly into his former misery. And added was the new fear of having been seen in the forest. He shuddered, and raised his hands to his face.

He heard again the noise that had woke him; it was a light thud, and seemed to be coming from upstairs. He jerked forward to the edge of the seat and put his head on one side to listen. It sounded again.

He rose quickly to his feet; it *was* coming from upstairs.

Footsteps. Undoubtedly footsteps. His top lip rose, his scalp tingled, and he strained to hear, counting the thuds. One . . . two . . . three . . .

They were light and muffled, but distinct; definitely coming from above, but at the same time having an echo of distance; nonchalant, but relentless. He clenched his fists and stared at the ceiling.

A door opened; he heard the hinge wail. His head shook in a sudden convulsion. Thud, thud, thud. He realized with a shiver of hope that it could be his wife, come home while he slept, and he shouted, 'Myra!' No answer. He shouted again, as loud as he could, 'MYRA!' No answer.

One . . . two . . . three . . . it was coming downstairs . . . four . . . five . . . six . . . with a harsh cry he whirled to face the hall door . . . seven . . . eight . . . nine . . . his brain refused to think of what it might be, could be . . . ten. . . .

He scrambled across the room and flung himself at the door and gripped the handle tightly. He'd have given anything for a strong bolt; or even a weak one.

Silence. He strained to listen, holding his precious breath and popping his eyes. The thuds had stopped; he could hear nothing other than the crepitation in his own ears. But he didn't ease his weight off the door.

There was another sound. This time coming from outside. Someone was coughing. He twisted his head and looked out of the window. Standing on the pavement, near the front of a car, was a man; portly, middle-aged, red-faced and white-headed. He was looking at the house next door.

With a melting sag of his body Bill realized that the footsteps had been coming from the other house, made by a prospective buyer who'd been looking it over and clumping around on the bare boards. He gazed with dreamy exhaustion out of the window and lifted a hand to his burning brow, and found it wet with sweat.

The man outside turned, caught his eye and waved. Bill blinked for a moment, surprised, then weakly returned the wave. The man swung fully about and started walking down toward the end of the street, obviously coming to the house.

Bill used his handkerchief to wipe his hands and face before going slowly into the hall. He was unable to resist shooting a glance to the top of the stairs, and looked back again as he opened the front door.

The man was leaning on the gatepost and staring solemnly into the garage. He turned his head quickly, and smiled. 'Ah, good day, sir.'

'Good day.' Bill went out on to the step. He was about to say he didn't know anything about the house next door when the man said:

'I was here yesterday, having a chat to your wife. I'm Detective-Sergeant Beedle.'

'Oh. Er—how do you do.'

'Howjado, Mr. Savage. Nice and fresh today.'

'Yes, it is. Er—was there something?'

'Well, we got a complaint at the station that some kids had been playing around the empty house there, so we got the key from the agent and came to have a look. Everything seems all right. I just wondered if you'd seen or heard any kids about.'

Bill shook his head. He knew for certain that never during the time the house had been vacant had any children been playing anywhere near it. He began to feel cold inside.

The detective smiled. 'Ah well. Probably a false alarm. Some people call the station if it rains.'

Bill tried to answer the smile, but didn't do too well. He nodded.

'But I wanted to have a chat with you, Mr. Savage, so it's not been a wasted journey.'

'Oh?'

'Nothing really. Just routine checking on that Clayton kidnapping.'

'Ah.'

'I wonder if you can remember where you were on Monday afternoon?'

Bill had to restrain himself from answering too quickly. He asked, 'Monday afternoon?'

'Yes. It was the seventeenth.'

'I remember. I was here. I didn't go out at all that day.'

'Ah. Anyone call?'

'Er—no. I don't think so. No.'

'It's just to verify that you were at home, you know.'

'Well, no, no one called.'

Beedle smiled. 'Oh, don't worry about it, Mr. Savage. We ask everyone these questions.'

'Of course. It's an awful thing, this kidnapping.'

'It is indeed.'

'Er—anything new?'

'No, I don't think there's been any new developments.' He turned his head as he spoke. Bill followed his gaze and saw a constable leaving the house next door. The constable shook his head at the detective, and went to the car and climbed in.

'Found nothing, apparently,' Beedle said, then glanced

into the garage. 'Your wife tells me you were out for a bit of fresh air yesterday, Mr. Savage. Go far, did you?'

'No. I—er—just went for a spin.'

'Out for the day?'

'No, I was back for, ah, just before noon.'

Beedle smiled at the bike. 'She's seen better days.'

'Yes.'

'Had her out today?'

Bill didn't know how to answer. For ten seconds he just stared at the detective, then quickly, to delay, started to cough deeply, turning his face to the side.

'Bit chesty?'

'Asthma,' Bill gasped. 'Very bad today.'

'Oh, you won't have been out then.'

Bill shook his head, now struggling with a real cough, brought on by the pretended one.

'Well, I won't keep you, Mr. Savage. It's chilly stood about.' He glanced in again at the bike, and turned away. 'Good day, sir. Thank you for your time.'

Bill nodded, and moved to the gatepost and leaned on it to finish coughing. When he straightened up, his eyes streaming from his effort and the agony in his lungs, he saw the police car turning the corner at the top of the street. A moment later Myra appeared from around the same corner, looking back over her shoulder. Bill walked slowly into the house. He sat down, used his atomizer, and leaned forward with his elbows on the chair arms and his shoulders hunched.

Myra came in, slamming the doors behind her, and crossed quickly to the hearth. She said, 'Was that the police?'

'Yes.'

'Mr. Laughing Beedle?'

Bill nodded, and told her the gist of the conversation. She listened carefully, and began taking off her coat. She said, 'I do not think there is anything to worry about.'

He blinked at her. 'But they're suspicious. Very suspicious.'

'Because of the empty house there? It is very likely that they did get a complaint. You know what people are for calling the police.'

'And the bike. He kept looking at the bike.'

'That does not mean anything. It has not been seen anywhere. Barnet, London or Epping. Has it?'

'Well . . . no.'

'They might realize that the tracks in the field at Barnet could have been made by a motor-cycle. But that is not proof.'

'But Epping. They saw me in the helmet and everything.'

'Even so, there must be half a million cyclists in and around London, and most of the helmets are white.'

Bill sighed and shook his head. 'He was suspicious. I could tell.'

'Well of course the police are suspicious. They are of everybody. That is their job. But suspicion is not proof.' She sat down in her chair. 'There is no way they can connect us with the Clayton child. You left no fingerprints in the car. You cannot be identified by Clayton or the chauffeur because of your disguise. All evidence that the child was ever here has been destroyed. The sheet and nightdress cannot be traced. And if they make inquiries about our activities of late they will find that they were quite normal. We bought the plywood, but now there is no longer anyone to describe the bedroom, that will not mean a thing. The chloroform we had had for years, and now that has been disposed of. Is there anything else?'

Bill stared miserably at the fire, and moved his head slowly and uncertainly from side to side.

Myra frowned at him and said, 'Tell me what happened in the woods.'

He told her about the three small Scouts, and the big one with whom he'd struggled, and the man who'd glanced up from his rubbish burning.

She said, 'That does not seem too bad. You had your goggles on all the time. I do not think we have anything to worry about. If the police were really suspicious they would have arrested us long ago and put us through a rigorous interrogation.'

'I suppose so.'

'Of course they would.' She rose and moved away from the hearth. 'I will make you a nice cup of tea.' Going into the kitchen she filled the kettle and set it on the stove, and began to hum softly. She wasn't too perturbed by the visit of the detective—she had implicit faith in her dream of immunity—and thought that under the circumstances things were going as well as could be expected. Also her talk with Mrs. Finch had rekindled the memory of her accomplishment at the séance the night before, lifting her spirits above their normal steady level.

Bill stared into the heart of the fire. He was filled with a strong foreboding of disaster.

Myra said, 'It is raining.' She was kneeling on the couch,

her forearms laid on its back and her chin on her clasped hands.

Bill, in his chair, nodded. Then, realizing she couldn't see the nod, said, 'Yes.'

'How is your chest?'

'Easier, thanks.'

'Sure you do not want anything to eat?'

'Yes, quite sure.'

'It is nearly four o'clock you know, and you had no breakfast.'

'I'm not hungry.'

Myra sighed. At any other time they would be eagerly discussing her latest supranormal experience. But Bill had hardly spoken all day, and then only if spoken to. She wondered how long it would take him to recover from the shock of the girl's death. He could not possibly be more despondent, she thought, if the child had been his own.

She turned her head and looked at his chair. 'I do wish you would try and pull yourself together. I fail to see why you should grieve so over someone else's child.'

Bill frowned, and shook his head slightly.

She asked, 'What did you say?'

'Nothing.'

She turned away, exasperated, and saw through the rain-streaked window that a car was splashing its way down the street. She said, 'There is a car coming.'

Bill eased tautly forward to the edge of the chair, turning his head to the side and waiting.

Myra said, 'It is coming here.'

Bill's hand rose to his throat, then to his mouth.

The car stopped at the gate. Myra put her face closer to the window, and said, 'It is a police car,' adding, as the car door opened and a man got out, 'and Detective-Sergeant Beedle.'

Bill twisted round, his face stricken. Myra looked at him sharply as she backed off from the couch. 'For God's sake, take hold of yourself. You look like a trapped animal.' But she felt uneasy herself as she went into the hall to answer the policeman's knock. She swung the door wide, smiling politely. 'Well, good day, Mr. Beedle.'

'Hello, Mrs. Savage. Here I am to trouble you again.'

'Please come in. Awful weather.'

'Thanks.' He stepped inside, running a hand over his glistening white hair. 'But we could do with a drop of rain.'

'I dare say.'

He said, smiling as usual, 'Well, I've come with a rather unusual request, sent on ahead as a sort of newsbreaker. Is your husband in?'

Myra frowned. 'Yes. Is it he you wished to speak to?'

'Not really, but I suppose I'd better explain the situation to you both.'

She opened the living-room door. 'This way, please.'

Bill rose slowly from his chair as they entered, hiding his trembling hands in his jacket pockets. He nodded at the detective, who asked, 'How's the old chest, Mr. Savage?'

'A bit better, thank you.'

'That's the way. Well now,' he said, sitting at Myra's gesture on the couch, 'first of all I must tell you that the Clayton girl has been found.'

Myra smiled. 'I knew it. I told Mrs. Clayton so.'

'Yes, but unfortunately the child is dead.'

'Dead!' Myra gasped, and sat down weakly at the table. Bill sat down too, and turned to the fire to hide his face.

Beedle said, 'She was found in Epping Forest about six hours ago.'

Myra shook her head. 'How dreadful.'

'Yes, a terrible thing.'

'What happened to her?'

'Well, the officers handling the case probably have a good idea how she died, but we don't know anything at this end. And of course there'll have to be an autopsy.'

There was a moment of silence, then the detective went on, 'Anyway, the thing is this. It seems that Charles Clayton wants to hold a séance here.'

Myra blinked. '*Mister* Clayton?'

'Yes. And I'm afraid that's all I can tell you about it. We simply got a call from Barnet to say that Mr. Clayton and Superintendent Watts of the Yard were on their way over, coming straight here to your house.'

'You mean now?'

'Yes. They should be here in ten or fifteen minutes. Apparently you told the Claytons that you'd be ready to help them at any time, but they asked us to send someone along to make sure you were available, and willing.'

'Why yes. Yes, it is quite all right. I am more than willing. But an afternoon séance is rather unusual.'

'But I believe, from what my wife says, that you are a bit unorthodox anyway.'

'Yes, that is quite true.'

Beedle grinned. 'You could call it a matinée séance.'

Myra smiled back. 'Of course.'

The detective turned to the hearth. 'I hope it won't be putting you out, Mr. Savage?'

'Oh no,' Bill said quickly, turning his head. 'No, it won't bother me.'

'Fine.' He looked at his watch. 'Well, they'll be here soon. Would it disturb you at all if I just waited here?' He looked from Myra to Bill and back again.

Myra said, 'Not in the least. Just make yourself at home. I will pop upstairs and get things ready.'

Bill rose. 'I'll give you a hand.'

They excused themselves and left the room. Myra trotted briskly up to the landing and stood waiting for Bill, who was coming slowly, on account of his asthma, holding the banister and touching the wall. They went into the box-room, crushing together to get the door closed.

With their faces no more than six inches apart, Bill hissed, 'I told you, I told you. They're suspicious.'

'It is possible that they are,' Myra said, keeping her voice low. 'And if so, this proves that they have absolutely nothing but those suspicions, and are hoping we will make a mistake and give ourselves away. In which case, of course, they would be disappointed. However, I am inclined to the other view.' She smiled. 'I think this is exactly what it appears to be. I think they really want my help. Clayton is now convinced of my powers. How could he be otherwise, after my predictions coming true?' Her smile widened. 'Tomorrow it will be in the papers that they came here.'

'But what'll you say at the séance?'

'I shall tell them mainly what they already know. I shall describe the blue bag and say it holds something of great value, and perhaps that it is being argued over. Then I shall say that it will be found within two days. In the morning you must take the money to the hut.'

Bill shook his head with short rapid movements, almost like a shiver. 'No. I can't do anything else. Don't ask me. I'm finished with it.'

She took hold of his elbows. 'For God's sake, man, get a grip on yourself. Have I not told you there is nothing to worry about.'

He bit his lip and grasped his hands tightly together.

She glared at him, and went on, 'I shall also give them vague descriptions of the kidnappers. Two or three men, evil-looking, swarthy, wearing rough clothes. It will be quite simple.'

'Perhaps,' he said, putting his head on one side, screwing closed his eyes and raising the clasped hands to his chin, 'perhaps you could say it was the chauffeur.'

'Yes, that's them,' Beedle said, turning back from the window and rising. 'They mustn't have wasted time on the way. Wet roads, too.'

Myra joined him at the door and they went into the hall. Bill got up from his chair and moved to the far side of the table, where he could see out of the window at a better angle. Walking from a small black car were three men, merely blurs through the rain-streaked partly steamed glass. When they had passed from view, Bill, about to turn away, was startled to see three cars crawl to a stop directly across the street. He stared at them till the sound of voices in the hall drew him to the door to listen.

Beedle introduced himself to the three arrivals, then introduced them to Myra. But Myra heard only the name of the third man, Superintendent Watts; she ignored the other one and merely gave Clayton a vague nod. She was staring up at the tall slender Watts, yet not actually seeing him; not seeing the thin aesthetic fortyish face and deep piercing eyes; she saw simply a person with a powerful aura of supranormal awareness. His metagnomic gift was the most manifest she had ever come across, and she thought excitedly that the Plan's purpose was already being fulfilled. She sensed that unlike Clayton, Watts was conscious of his gift, and she could tell by the way his eyes repeatedly sought hers that he recognized her talent too.

She came aware that an awkward silence had fallen, and said, 'Oh, please go into the lounge.'

Bill had moved back from the door and was standing by the table, gripping the top of a chair. The five people came in and he was introduced to the newcomers. He couldn't keep his eyes off Clayton, who stood staring down at the carpet, his hands in his pockets. Bill was fascinated and horrified to see that Clayton's face was a definite shade of grey.

Superintendent Watts said, 'I believe you're not feeling too good today, Mr. Savage?'

Bill looked away from Clayton. 'Er—no. Asthma.'

'An awful complaint. You'll be out of work then, I suppose.'

'Oh yes.'

Myra said, 'It takes him all his time to climb the stairs.'

The tall man nodded, then said, 'I understand you worked as a cab driver at one time.'

Bill's grip on the chair tightened. 'Oh—er—yes, that's right. But many years ago.'

'In Barnet, wasn't it?'

'Er—yes.'

Clayton caused a diversion by turning away from the group and walking to the hearth, where he stood looking down into the fire. Bill kept his face toward him, hoping that this would change the tack of the conversation. It did. He heard Watts's smooth cultured voice say, 'I think you'll be interested to know, Mrs. Savage, that I'm the president of the Southern Society for Psychical Research.'

Myra said, 'Well, that certainly is interesting.'

Bill felt it was safe to turn back. He turned, and got a shock that made his knees wilt. The third of the newcomers was holding a hat in his hand; a green hat.

Bill turned away completely and fumbled around to the front of the chair he was gripping and sank into it. He leaned an elbow on the table and leaned his face on his hand. He tried to tell himself that green hats were as common as brown or grey ones, but he was unconvinced and had to cross his legs tightly to keep their shaking from being seen.

Myra was cheerfully talking shop. She said, 'Yes, I find the results of the Kroner experiments very significant. And I believe they have done some startling things in Austria.'

'That's true. I was over there last year, on my holidays, and I can tell you they're making great strides.'

'Have you read the . . .' Myra broke off, taken aback, as something bright flashed briefly in the street outside.

Watts glanced through the window. 'Oh, that's the reporters, taking pictures. I'm afraid you're going to find yourself in the newspapers, Mrs. Savage.'

Myra smiled. 'Oh well. I suppose we cannot stop them.'

'No indeed. Freedom of the Press, you know.'

Myra said, looking up at the tall man curiously, 'I find it difficult to believe that someone so traditionally—um—shall we say "hard-headed" as a policeman would be interested in psychical research. Most people with methodical minds ridicule the idea of discarnate agency and laugh the whole thing off as mumbo-jumbo.'

'Well, Mrs. Savage, I wouldn't go so far as to say I accept communication with the dead as fact. Nor do I discount its possibility. I look at it, perhaps because I am a policeman, in the way the Law looks at a man charged with a crime. The Law says a man is innocent till proven guilty. I say discarnate agency is not a fact till proved so, and in the meantime keep an open mind.'

Myra said, 'It is a pity more people do not take that sensible stand.'

'Yes, but so many have had dealings with phony mediums, or read about mediums being unmasked as phonies, that it's no wonder they sneer at the whole thing. And the people who know nothing at all about psychical research think that it's some sort of religion.'

Myra nodded, smiling. She was warming more and more to the man. She said, 'Well, your attitude explains the request for a séance. It struck me as strange that the police would want to try this method of getting information.'

'Actually,' Watts said, glancing toward the man at the hearth, 'it was Mr. Clayton's idea. After what you told his wife last night, and told him on the phone this morning, he was determined to come here as soon as possible. They got hold of me—I wasn't connected with the case until today—and asked me to step in and come along with Mr. Clayton.'

'I see. I certainly hope your journey will be justified.'

'I'm sure you'll do your best, Mrs. Savage.'

'I will. Shall we start then?'

'Yes, we might as well.'

Myra looked at Beedle and the other policeman, both of whom had been standing silently by. 'And these two gentlemen also?'

Watts said, 'No, I don't think so. I'd like to have just you and your husband and Clayton and me. With your permission.'

'Yes. But my husband is not a regular sitter.'

'Oh, I don't think that that matters.'

'Very well.'

Watts turned to the man with the green hat, and asked, 'Do you suppose you could get the station on the car radio from here?'

'Well,' the man said, looking at his questioner closely, 'I can't say for certain.'

'You don't know?'

'I'm not positive, sir.'

'But you think it possible?'

'Well, yes. But I couldn't say for sure.'

'I see.'

The significance of this exchange was lost on Myra, but not on Bill. He'd been listening closely. He knew the Superintendent had been asking the detective if he could positively identify the collector of the ransom money. He pressed his knuckles against his teeth, not at all relieved by the detective's indecision.

Watts said, 'Anyway, I think you two men can wait outside.'

Beedle and the man with the green hat both murmured, 'Yes, sir,' and left the room. Myra asked the Superintendent if he would like to take off his coat, and while he was doing just that she went to Clayton with the same question. Clayton turned from the fire, blinking. Then he nodded and began to remove his overcoat. Myra thought he had aged since she'd last seen him. His eyes were heavy and the whites badly shot with blood, and his jowls seemed to have loosened and gone flabby. She took the coat from him, and he spoke for the first time since entering the house: 'Thank you.' She hesitated, wondering whether or not she should offer condolences, but decided not to and turned away. She lay both garments on the couch and opened the door. 'If you will come with me, please.'

They went into the hall, the hostess leading and the host slowly following, and up the stairs. The window in the séance room was already covered, and Myra put a match to the candle. She took four chairs to the table and arranged her sitters: Bill facing her, Watts on her left and Clayton on the right.

Very little daylight came through or around the window blind, and what did was overpowered by the candle, which glowed warmly on every face and threw four slightly shifting shadows on the walls. The fall of the rain could be faintly heard, and its gurgle as it ran along the gutter.

Myra said, 'Let us make a circle.'

They joined hands, Bill having to lay his forearms along the table to grip with Clayton and Watts. Clayton's hand was cold.

Myra fixed her gaze just above the point of the candle flame. She had already decided what to do. Not wanting to waste the opportunity of sitting with two paranormals, one as powerful as the Superintendent, she thought she would first go into trance and see what happened. After that she could come back to normal and say anything she wished.

She concentrated hard on making her mind a thoughtless blank, putting aside every immediate problem and object and person, even herself, and soon her consciousness was rising into a zone beyond spatial and temporal laws. Her eyelids drooped, her mouth slackened, and she was moving. . . .

The friendly, gentle, sympathetic yellow of the walls in the corridor made her smile and lifted her state to a level of eye-tingling happiness, and drew her irresistibly to the door; drew her at a much swifter pace than usual, as though a new strength had been augmented. She glided smoothly on, and the door grew rapidly till it was a mere breath's length away. She stopped, and her heart stopped too. Her soul yearned forward, straining, pleading. Then the white knob began to turn slowly. Her heart started beating, faster than before, and she knew with a great upsurge of elation that she was about to go into the room once again. The door swung in, smoothly and with a heavy graduality, and a humming sound that was almost music oozed out like hot air. She went forward, into a dusky light and a protective motherly warmth, and immediately her being soared to an ecstatic perfection. She stopped, and stood gazing around, her arms out, watching the room appear as the light slowly strengthened. Periodless pieces, chairs, tables, a low couch, everything simple yet luxurious, a rocking horse, voluptuous drapes on vaguely patterned walls without windows, lamps shaded by parchment and glass, a crib, a candelabra, a black-red floor-covering, an up-stood silk-lined casket, a mammoth carved ebony cabinet full of moonlight-blue pottery, a piano-like instrument at whose keyboard, her back turned, sat a woman in a flowing gown of gold, a gold barely distinguishable from the waist-length hair, and beyond the woman an open french window, and through it a gently swirling light grey mist. She swept her eyes over every detail, hungrily affirming that nothing was changed, and arrived finally with her gaze on the window, longingly. She had never been that far; she had never been farther than the spot she now occupied. But, as she looked, she found herself moving again, moving forward toward the window, and as she went the woman at the keyboard began to turn. As they drew closer together she saw, with complete understanding and immediate acceptance, that the woman had no face. She went on, and halted at the threshold of the window. There was now a faint, pleasant, sensuous smell of something burning. The mist floated lazily before her, so close she could have touched it, and through it was a feel of space unlimited. She tried to move on. It was difficult. Something pushed at the sides; yet something pulled from the front; it was like being forced through a small and slippery opening. With a sudden release that sent her a leap's length forward she was out in the mist. She went straight ahead, hearing now a gentle sighing, as if a million mouths were drawing air. A tree trunk loomed in front. But coming close she saw that it was not a tree but something that hung from above and coiled on the ground; it was off-white and indented here and there; it looked like a giant umbilical cord. She put out a hand and touched it, and immediately her other hand was grasped and a convulsion ran through her. . . .

Bill wasn't sure whether or not his wife was acting. Her eyes were closed and her mouth was partly open. She looked as she always did in real or make-believe trance: pleasantly asleep.

Suddenly she stiffened, her lips moved, and she made a hoarse monotonic sound. After a brief pause she made another sound, of a higher pitch, then another still higher. Her mouth opened and closed, silently forming words. Then she relaxed a little, and said in a hoarsely high voice:

'Is that you, Daddy?'

A tremor passed around the table. A cold claw scrambled up Bill's spine and his hair moved, and he almost cried out as his left hand was gripped tightly by Clayton.

'I can't see very well. I think it's a frosted window.'

Watts was leaning a little to one side, intent on Myra's face.

'It's very nice . . . I think. . . . Nicer than before. I didn't like it before. I was in a horrible old hospital. . . . Yes? . . . Yes?'

Clayton's mouth had sagged open and he was staring wide-eyed, unblinking, at the candle flame.

'But I wish I could see better. It's all milky. . . . What? Is someone crying?'

Watts leaned closer to Myra and said, almost whispered, 'What happened when you left school?'

'School? When I left school? . . . Oh yes. It was funny. No, it was awful. . . . Ooh, look at that. . . .'

Watts said, his eyes still boring into Myra's face, 'What was awful?'

'A man. A horrible man. He made me blow my nose. A big fat man, I think. And then there was the hospital. That was very horrible. And then there was an aeroplane. No, a cabinet. Very special. It made me sick. . . .'

The grip on Bill's hand was so tight that he didn't know how much longer he could go on without doing something about it.

'Oh, and I broke the dishes all over the floor. But she didn't say anything, the nurse. I thought she would. She did before. She hit me an' hit me, and said she'd beat me if I was bad. . . . I wasn't bad. I'm never bad. . . . She's French. She said it was a secret, but I don't care. She's French. . . . No, I'm busy now.'

Watts asked, 'Where was the hospital?'

'I don't know. I had a room of my own. It was always cold. And there was no window.'

Bill had forgotten the pain in his hand. He was staring at Myra and wondering just how close she would go to the truth. She was too close already.

'I wish I had Bimbo and Peter with me. But it doesn't matter. . . . Yes, isn't it nice?'

Clayton's head was trembling like that of a palsied ancient, and from his sagging lower lip a thin thread of spittle was slowly lowering its blobbed end.

Watts said, 'Where did you go after you left the hospital?'

'Is my daddy there?'

'Where did you go after you left the hospital? A house?'

'I don't know. I was there a long time. With that Frenchy and the man. Not the big fat man with black hair. Another one.'

'What did he look like?'

'Very thin. And she was thin too.'

Bill was staring with amazement at Myra. He thought, could it possibly be . . .?

'What did the woman look like?' asked Watts.

'Oh, just thin. Dressed in white. She's a nurse. I didn't like her. She hit me.'

'Did the man hit you?'

'No, but he wouldn't let me shout when I heard Mummy's voice in the next room. I know she'd come to see me and he wouldn't let me shout to her. He was looking at her through a little hole under a picture.'

Fascinated, petrified, Bill stared at his wife, not feeling the pain that came now from both tightly gripped hands.

'He didn't hit me, but she did. She's got a nasty face, and there's a star painted on her forehead. I think she's a spy. I could hear her talking in the next room, to Mummy. But I couldn't shout. He held his hand over my mouth and I couldn't breathe. I couldn't breathe at all. It was terrible. I thought I was going to die, really I did. . . . But it was all right. . . . There they go again. So pretty.'

Bill jerked his head a little to one side as he suddenly came aware that Watts was leaning close to him. He blinked into the policeman's face, which had a very faint smile curling about the mouth and which seemed somehow benevolent, and felt all his fear begin to drain away.

Watts said, 'Where's the money, Mr. Savage?'

Bill said, 'In the kitchen.'

'But the cabinet was funny. It was just like an aeroplane, only a small one. It made an awfully big noise, the same as a motor-bike, and swayed about all over the place. . . .'

Bill was consumed by a tremendous feeling of relief. Without thinking he pulled his hands free and pressed them to his cheeks.

'And there was another . . . Oh. . . .'

Myra's face twisted with a grimace of pain and sorrow. She sobbed. Her head sank forward and moved slowly from side to side.

Watts let go of her hand and rose from the table. He went to the door and switched on the light, then turned and leaned against the wall. Pulling out a handkerchief he wiped his brow and lips.

The rain was heavier. It drummed on the window and tinkled into the metal trough just above it. The sound was peaceful; it matched perfectly Bill's feeling of exhausted release. He felt free, and safe, and wanted more than anything to go to sleep.

Myra gasped and opened her eyes, and seemed to shrink into herself. Her face expressed anguish. She looked dazedly around the room, and at the man sat holding her hand.

Clayton's head had been turning slowly, and now he was gazing at Myra; gazing open-mouthed and with sorrowing, puzzled eyes. He held on firmly when she tried to withdraw her hand.

She began again to look around the room. Her expression gradually changed to wonder, then to astonishment, then to amazement, and then to joy; but hesitant joy.

She swung her eyes on her husband and stared at him. 'Tell me,' she gasped. 'Tell me. Did I do it?'

Bill nodded, and smiled gently. 'Yes. You did it.'

MYSTERIOUSPRESS.COM

Otto Penzler, owner of the Mysterious Bookshop in Manhattan, founded the Mysterious Press in 1975. Penzler quickly became known for his outstanding selection of mystery, crime, and suspense books, both from his imprint and in his store. The imprint was devoted to printing the best books in these genres, using fine paper and top dust-jacket artists, as well as offering many limited, signed editions.

Now the Mysterious Press has gone digital, publishing ebooks through **MysteriousPress.com**.

MysteriousPress.com offers readers essential noir and suspense fiction, hard-boiled crime novels, and the latest thrillers from both debut authors and mystery masters. Discover classics and new voices, all from one legendary source.

FIND OUT MORE AT

WWW.MYSTERIOUSPRESS.COM

FOLLOW US:

@emysteries and Facebook.com/MysteriousPressCom

MysteriousPress.com is one of a select group of publishing partners of Open Road Integrated Media, Inc.